DESTINY

EDMANTHA HALL

SAGEBRUSH PUBLISHING

CANTON, TEXAS

Edmantha Hall/Sagebrush Publishing
Printed in the United States of America
edmanthahallbooks.com

Destiny/ Edmantha Hall. -- 1st ed.

ISBN 978-1985859135 Print Edition

Also by Edmantha Hall

The Human Megmador

Sacrificial Child

I am dedicating this book to my loving sister, Melissa Hall: 03/02/1942-09/15/2013,
and to my wonderful brother, Edmantha Hall: 03/13/1948-4/22/2014,
whose pen name I used for my book.

Chapter 1

New Orleans, 1853

A POWERFUL STORM hammered New Orleans late that April, bringing a torrent of rainwater cascading from the rooftops, overflowing rivers and streams, and flooding the swamps. All fieldwork had stopped for two weeks due to the heavy rainfall, and the slaves got a break from their hard labor. Floodwater washed away most of the seeds and plants, ruining crops, so the slaves would have to replant.

The sun was shining. Muddy puddles started to disappear, and swollen streams had stopped overflowing their banks, but the ground was still saturated.

Mary took a good look at herself in a broken mirror that morning. She had blonde, curly hair she'd inherited from her father and brown eyes from her mother. She'd used this old mirror to pin up her hair in various styles. She usually kept her long locks pulled to one side in a thick braid. She stood at a medium height, two inches taller than her half-sister, Becky.

Without her parents' knowledge, Becky had secretly taught Mary how to read and write when they were younger. Mary and Becky were born three months apart, with Becky being the elder. Both were sixteen now. They had been the closest of friends until Becky discovered that Mary was her father's slave child. Becky was not as pretty as Mary, but she'd inherited her blue eyes from her father and brown hair from her mother, who was now deceased. Mary's half-sister despised her because she looked prettier and whiter than she did. Becky hated Mary so much she refused to allow her to remain her personal maid.

Master Boyd owned the plantation and was father to both girls. He lent Mary out to work for their nearest neighbor, a widow named Mrs. Thatcher.

Master Boyd's slaves grew cotton, sugar cane, and an assortment of vegetables. Some ended up on the New Orleans docks and traveled north up the Mississippi. Cotton was shipped to the East Coast or to Europe.

"Mary," Josh called, "time to go." Josh was an old slave with gray hair and wrinkled, charcoal-colored skin. He drove a wagon all day, taking lunch to the slaves and driving others back and forth.

Mary was the oldest of her mother's four children, and she roomed with her twelve-year-old sister, Iris. Her three-year-old brother shared a room with their eight-year-old brother. Her oldest brother worked in the stables with his father, Walter, feeding the animals. Master Boyd allowed her mother and stepfather to live together as husband and wife, although they weren't married. Mary couldn't force herself to call him Daddy, as her siblings did.

Dashing out the front door, she rushed to the wagon and jumped up on the seat with Josh.

"Morning, Mary," Josh said. "You sure like working for Mrs. Thatcher, don't you?" He shook the horse's reins. "Git up, old girl."

"She's a nice lady," Mary replied. The wagon lurched into motion, and Mary was off to her dream world. She pulled on a homemade bonnet and giggled, tying the strings under her chin. She couldn't tell Josh that Mrs. Thatcher was allowing her to practice reading and helping her with her figures. She was also teaching Mary how to speak proper English, as the ladies did in the East. Someday, in the near future, Mary planned to escape to New York City and live as a free white woman. Mrs. Thatcher gave her a reason to live—something to look forward to in life. Although she and Mrs. Thatcher never talked about her going East one day, it was a silent understanding between them. The woman was prepping Mary for a new future.

Josh chuckled. "Seems like you can't wait to get over there."

***

Mrs. Thatcher's two-story mansion sat about a quarter of a mile from the main road. It looked similar to other Southern plantation homes, painted white, with big pillars that held up the front porch. A well-manicured lawn, magnolia trees, roses, and other fine flowers accented the yard. The old woman was in her mid-sixties with shoulder-length gray hair. She had smooth, soft-looking skin for a woman her age. She'd given up farming and sold off most of her slaves after her husband died eight years earlier. Only four slaves remained to take care of her place.

An elderly maid, Hattie May, was supposed to take care of the household, but she was too old to even take care of herself. During Mary's visits, she rarely saw the woman, because Hattie May spent most of the time in her room sleeping. Mrs. Thatcher probably kept her because she had been her children's maid, and she loved the woman's company. The only other people living there were three men who maintained the yard, the transportation, and the stables. Her daughter had moved to New York City, her son to Philadelphia.

Unlike other slaves, Mrs. Thatcher allowed Mary to walk right through her front door. She knocked gently, entered, and yelled, "Mrs. Thatcher?"

"I'm in the kitchen, honey," the old lady replied.

Walking through the fine living room, as Mary had many times, she felt that she deserved such fancy riches in her life. One day she would have them, just like Mrs. Thatcher. Similar to Master Boyd's house, the dining area and living room were large enough to accommodate many guests. However, Mrs. Thatcher never had callers. Mary entered the expansive kitchen, where she found the woman sitting at a small table usually occupied by house slaves, drinking tea and eating toast and scrambled eggs.

"Mrs. Thatcher," Mary said, "I could have cooked that for you. Do you want me to show up earlier in the future?"

"No, dear. My eyesight is getting worse. I can't wait to have you read to me."

Mary smiled knowingly. "Another romance novel?"

"Yes. You know how much I love those stories, and you've learned how to read so well—pronounce your words like a proper lady, not like these Southern Belles. My books are hard to find here in New Orleans. The women around here consider them trash, so I have to order most from back East."

"Why don't you move East like your children did? Your husband is gone, and you have nothing to keep you here."

"I'm too old to make the move. I've been here for over forty years. This old house has too many memories."

"You're not that old. In fact, you look very young for being in your mid-sixties, Mrs. Thatcher. You live like me. No friends here. Why?"

"Something that happened years ago. The local women still shun me for it."

"That's an even better reason to leave this place."

"Maybe that's why I live my life through books," Mrs. Thatcher said.

Mary thoroughly cleaned one room per month and spent most of her time talking and reading to Mrs. Thatcher. She picked up the book next to the old woman. "Mysterious Admirer?" She loved these stories as much as Mrs. Thatcher did.

The woman giggled like a teenager. "I can't wait for you to read it to me, Mary."

Mary opened the book to the first page and began reading. After finishing half the book, they retired to the backyard. The old woman didn't sit in the screened-in gazebo but relaxed under a magnolia tree. She sat in a lounge chair, ate two chocolate cookies, and sipped her tea. Then she started telling Mary stories about New York City and other Eastern places she'd visited when she was young.

Before long, Josh was calling Mary. She had been asking him to fetch her later and later each day. She didn't want to leave Mrs. Thatcher's side. She wished the old woman would make a deal with Master Boyd and purchase her, but that never happened. Mary would love to be Mrs. Thatcher's slave.

She cheerfully left Mrs. Thatcher's house with a five-dollar bill in her pocket and some of Mrs. Thatcher's daughter's old things in a canvas bag. When Mary arrived home, she hopped off the wagon and ran toward her house. Her heart was thumping like a drum. They didn't have a living room, as white folks did, so her parents slept in the front room. When she rushed in, her mother and stepfather were sitting in chairs. Her eight-year-old brother was resting on the bed, holding his little brother in his lap, and her sister sat on the opposite side.

Her mother stood as Mary entered. "Why are you spending so much time at Mrs. Thatcher's house? Josh said you asked him to pick you up later than usual. What's in the bag?"

Mary pulled out two dresses, a hat, and a pair of shoes. "Mrs. Thatcher gave them to me," she said, breathless. "Aren't they the loveliest things?" She held one of the dresses up to herself and twirled around in front of her family.

"And where are you going to wear them, Cinderella? To the ball?" her mother asked.

Her stepfather, Walter, hated white folks—and also hated the sight of her because she didn't look black like the rest of his family. Her sister and brothers were his children, and he treated Mary differently—coldly.

"It's bad enough you look like 'em," he said to her. "Now you're talking like 'em. What's next, dressing like 'em? Look, miss fancy white girl, your mother is black, which makes you black. You'll never fit into their society. The only reason men ain't studding you now is because Master Boyd won't let 'em. A wench is all you'll ever be good for in this world. You'd better know your place, or you're going to get us whipped or hanged one day."

Heat flashed throughout Mary's body as she turned to Walter. "The only reason you have a soft job is because of Master Boyd. I'm his child, and he sees to me the best he can. We have a house instead of living in the slave quarters, and my little sister doesn't have to work like other girls her age. You and Mama live together as husband and wife because of me. My brothers and sister know who their parents are. They're not sold off to the highest bidder like cows." She screamed, "I demand you show me a little more respect."

The slap across Mary's left cheek burned like a raging inferno as she landed hard on the floor. She couldn't hold back her tears.

Walter yanked her up by the arm.

"You talk to me like that again, gal, and that white ass of yours will be so red you won't be able to sit for a week. Get all these notions out your head about living white and moving East." He pointed a stiff finger at the door. "Now get out of here. I'm sick of looking at you."

Mary ran out the back door and sat on the steps, grimacing. A short distance away, willows at the creek swayed in the gentle wind. The water always brought her peace, but not today. Nothing would solace the pain in her heart. She felt so alone in the world. The blacks hated her because she looked white, and the whites hated her because she was black. Master Boyd had kids by other slaves, but they didn't have fair skin, as she did.

Mary despised going to the slave quarters. The

structure consisted of many crudely made buildings with dirt floors, no windows, and single walls. There was one group of buildings for the men and another for the women and children. Each slave had their own cot with all their personal belongings stuffed underneath it. The occupants always stared and whispered as she neared. None of them were friendly.

Mary had never had a friend, and the other slaves envied her and her family because of the preferential treatment they received from Master Boyd. The slave quarters were about a fourth of a mile behind the big two-story mansion. Mary's house was a four-room shack tucked among pine trees all by itself, about halfway between the master's house and the slave quarters.

Today, her mind was heavily preoccupied. With her head down, she fingered a pleat on her dress. Deep in thought, she didn't notice Jimmy until she glanced up. Not wanting to deal with him today, she rolled her eyes.

Jimmy was Master Boyd's son by his second wife. He was nearly eight years old and was Mary's half-brother, but he'd never know it. Mary was a slave, and she wasn't considered a relative but an animal. If he had known that Mary was his half-sister, it would have created more tension between them. Jimmy often wandered around their house, tormenting her. He had blond hair and blue eyes like his father. Today, he was shirtless and barefoot.

"Hey, you witch," he yelled at her. Jimmy picked up a handful of small rocks and threw them at her, one by

Master Boyd owned lots of land. Some he didn't farm. Instead, he used it to raise cows and horses. It would take Cyris two days to walk around the entire plantation.

Master Boyd had purchased Cyris when he was just six years old. His old master told him to keep his left hand in his pocket so no one would see the burn scar. He had been serving coffee in the big house when he'd spilled some on a woman's beautiful dress. For his punishment, they had stuck his hand into a pot of boiling water and then whipped him. His old master said he was no good.

As long as he worked, he'd never had a problem at Master Boyd's plantation. The burned hand never hindered him from working, and the scar was barely visible today. When his old master had taken him from his mother, he was too young to remember her name or her face. He had two brothers and three sisters but couldn't remember their names either.

Before sundown, the fieldwork stopped for the day. Cyris hoped supper was good, because he was hungry and exhausted.

At the slave quarters, Cyris grabbed a hot meal of pig's feet, corn bread, turnip greens, and mashed potatoes. Today he had sassafras tea rather than milk. As most slaves did, he headed straight to bed after his meal. He had to be up early the next morning for another hard day's work. If he got home early, he'd walk along the creek, which wasn't too far from his quarters. He liked looking at the water where it churned around a fallen tree that nearly reached the other side. He'd love to dive into the stream, but he didn't know how to swim. Other than Jimmy, he'd never seen anyone swim.

All the snoring from the other men never kept Cyris awake at night. He always fell asleep as soon as his head hit the pillow. The smell of a hot breakfast usually woke him up every morning. Getting in line with the other men, he received a plate of food and a glass of milk. It came straight from the cow, still warm.

***

That day, Cyris climbed into Josh's wagon early, just after sunup. When he got a glimpse of Mary, she was hanging out clothes. Everyone knew her name, because her family lived in a house all by themselves. She looked like a white girl with blonde hair and skin fairer than most white folks. None of the slaves talked to her. Although she too was a slave, no one seemed to care for her or anyone in her family. Mary was idle most of the time, it seemed. Although her sister was old enough to work, she never did. That infuriated the rest of the slaves. Mary's family got special treatment—not because she was Master Boyd's bastard child, but because she looked white. He'd had children by other slave women, but Mary was different. She simply didn't look black.

One day, Cyris would muster up enough courage to talk to her.

***

"There she is," a woman on the back of the wagon announced.

"Yeah," another woman said. "Don't see her working in the fields."

"She's too good to work. I've heard she goes to the Widow Thatcher's house and dollies around all day, keeping the woman company, drinking tea, and talking."

"Where did you hear that?" the other woman asked.

"From Jimmy. Miss Becky doesn't like her either, and she has asked her father on many occasions to put her to work with us."

"Doesn't she know Mary's her half-sister?" Josh asked.

"That's why Becky hates her. Standing next to Mary, Becky looks like a sow." Both women laughed.

"I'd had three kids by the time I was her age."

"I had four."

"She's something special, all right. Wonder what Master Boyd's planning to do with her. Surely no white man will marry her."

"Just look at her. She thinks she's better than us."

Josh listened to the complaints and came to Mary's defense. "She's a nice girl."

"Why aren't we nice?"

"Because you gossip about people," Josh said.

"If we hadn't had men studding us since we were nine years old, maybe we'd look pretty too."

"Or if we hadn't been working like horses," the other woman said.

"I've had two kids by Master Boyd. He never gave me any special privileges. He sold my kids off, as if he didn't even know them."

Josh looked straight ahead. "Irene, none of us wants to be here. I'm sorry you've had a hard life. We all have."

Cyris again thought about how he planned to get to know Mary. Although not formally introduced, he had delivered groceries to her home a few times and hoped she remembered him. With all the time she spent at the widow's house, she must know something worth learning. He didn't want to be a slave all his life, but he'd never heard anything about freedom. If there was a way to liberty, he felt that Mary would know.

Cyris worked hard, hoeing until lunch. Josh served them ham sandwiches and lemonade right there at their worksite. If anyone had to use the bathroom, they hid behind a cotton stalk, which didn't offer much privacy. There was no place to wash their hands either, even before eating.

That day, they finished the fieldwork and went home earlier than usual. Before supper, Cyris walked along the creek. It was his solitude ... getting away from the crowded slave quarters. Jimmy was there swimming. He thought the boy was too young to be out there all alone. He could have an accident, and there would be no one to rescue him. Jimmy saw him, but they didn't acknowledge each other. Cyris wanted to be alone, so he left the boy uninterrupted.

Chapter 3

May 1853

JOE JOE WAS head of the overseers. Mary hated the way he ogled her with lust in his eyes. He was medium height, about forty, and big. His pants were too large, but they fit tightly around his waist. His hair was thinning, but he had a full, black beard. The fat slob had his way with any of the slave women he wanted, except for Mary. He took orders directly from the master, and Mary was off limits.

Mary walked past the big house with an empty basket. Pokeweeds grew wild on the edge of the estate. She wore a bonnet and an old hand-me-down pink dress. She was staring at the ground and didn't have a chance to change her direction of travel until she was close to five dirty, foul-smelling men standing under a shade tree, drinking water from canteens.

Joe Joe blocked her path. "Hey, pretty girl. Can I walk with you?"

Mary despised him, wanted to see him die. "No. Leave me alone."

"Now, why would a pretty little thing like you want to be left alone?"

Just the idea of him touching her made Mary flinch. She wanted to gouge out his eyes. "I'm working, and I don't want to be bothered."

"Why don't I help you? My, don't that basket look heavy. Want me to carry it?"

"Go away."

She tried to go around him, but he blocked her path again.

"You're not very friendly, are you?" he asked, pulling something from his shirt pocket. "I have a nice necklace here for you. Pure gold. This would look mighty pretty around your neck." He dangled the cheap trinket in Mary's face and then snatched it back. "If'n you nice to me, I'll give it to you, and a five-dollar bill too. Bet you've never had money before, have you? You can buy things with it. Just meet me at those willows," he pointed toward the creek, "in a little while."

"I'd rather die."

He nodded. "You just might."

The three slaves and a young white overseer named Mike grinned as if they had just won a hundred dollars.

She hated Mike almost as much as she hated Joe Joe. He was shorter and much younger than Joe Joe. Married just two months earlier, he'd visited her house when her folks were away, stormed in, and wrestled her to the floor. After she dug her fingernails into his penis, he'd let out a scream and let her go. Her mother had informed her of how sensitive men's genitals were, and this knowledge saved her virginity that day.

Mary growled out, "If you have this conversation with me again, I'll personally tell Master Boyd."

A red-faced frown replaced his sly grin. "I'm going to get you, girl, and soon."

Mary feared that one day either Joe Joe or Mike would succeed in raping her. Both frightened her, and she had tried to keep her distance as best she could.

Joe Joe and Mike hated each other, and Joe Joe was on Mike's back every chance he got. Mary didn't hear the disagreement between the two rivals as she picked poke salad greens that day, but an argument had broken out. Mary heard lots of shouting and screaming as she completed her task. As she neared the group, she couldn't help but stare as Joe Joe beat Mike senseless before the other men broke up the fight.

"I'm going to kill you, Joe Joe," Mike threatened from a split lip. He wiped the blood from his chin, retrieved his hat, smacked it against his leg, and put it on his head.

Mike had dropped his knife during the struggle. It was about nine inches long and enclosed in a leather sheath. Seeing the weapon lying there, Mary stood with her dress covering it. When no one was looking, she picked it up and hid it in her basket. She had a plan, but it might get her hanged if she was caught.

"What's going on out here?" Master Boyd shouted. He was a slender man with a thick head of blond hair who stood about five feet ten inches.

"We had a disagreement, suh," Joe Joe answered.

"I don't want to see any more disagreements like this here again. Is that clear?"

"Yes, suh," Joe Joe promised.

"Mike, don't you and these men have something better to do?"

"Yes, suh," Mike said. He rubbed his thin mustache with the back of his index finger. "Let's go to work, boys." He walked off, and the three slaves followed him.

Joe Joe glanced at Mary and smiled as if he'd just won a prize fight.

Master Boyd ignored Mary as if she didn't exist.

She walked back to her house and changed into her black dress.

Anxiously watching out her front window, Mary saw Joe Joe walking toward the slave quarters. She removed Mike's knife from its sheath, hid it under her dress, rushed out to intercept Joe Joe, and then slowed her pace as she neared him. She sashayed over to him and said in a sexy voice, "Mr. Joe Joe. I really liked the way you handled yourself back there. You're a real man. How about that necklace you promised me and ten dollars if I meet you at the creek?"

He blushed. "You go ahead. I'll meet you there in about ten minutes."

Mary walked toward the creek. Glancing over her shoulder, she smiled at the fool who thought he was about to get lucky. When Mary reached the creek, she followed a trail until it ended, just past where a fallen tree lay in the stream. She thoroughly scanned the area with her eyes, making sure no one else was around. She was totally alone. Her entire body shook, and her legs became so weak she had to sit on the ground.

When Joe Joe arrived, Mary had the knife concealed under her dress. He fell to his knees, placed thick-callused hands on either side of her cheeks, puckered his lips, and planted a sloppy kiss on her mouth. His eyes glimmered with lustful desire, and his thick beard tickled her face.

"I knew I'd get you. Don't tell anyone you met me. You are so beautiful. Can't believe you're black. Why, you could pass for a white woman any day of the week."

Mary clutched the knife with a shaking hand and held it under her dress. "Where's my necklace and the ten dollars you promised?"

He dropped the necklace in her lap, pulled out a wad of cash from his back pocket, and dropped a dollar bill on the ground next to her. He didn't believe in banks, and everyone knew he carried a large sum of money on his person.

"Ten dollars," he said.

She had to have the courage to go through with her plan because she knew that at this point, if she tried to back out, he would rape her. Mary jumped to her knees, pulled the knife from under her dress, and stabbed him in his genital area. All the hate and frustration were expunging from her body as her hands shook out of control.

"I hate you, you fat pig. Don't you think I know the difference between a dollar and a ten-dollar bill?" Mary wanted him out of her life, wanted to be free from his harassment, knowing that someday soon neither Joe Joe or Mike would get a chance to rape her.

Then, finding strength she didn't know she had, she stabbed his upper torso and neck until she was exhausted. "You're not getting anything from me." Leaving the knife wedged into his chest, she pulled the wad of cash from his pocket and also took his watch.

There was no one else at the creek, so no one would know what had just happened.

She removed the top of the rotten stump, placed the money into the box she'd hidden there, and put the top back in place. The stump was off the worn path, so no one would think of looking there. After washing the blood from her face and hands, she fled the area, walking from the verdant willows and into the sunlight.

When someone found Joe Joe's body with Mike's knife wedged in his chest, Mike was the first and only suspect. She'd heard later that the authorities arrested him and charged him with Joe Joe's murder, but she didn't keep up with the rumor mill.

Two out of her three worst nightmares were out of her life forever, and she was richer for it.

CHAPTER 4

MARY GOES TO TOWN

MARY'S MOTHER SOMETIMES worked at the big house. Mrs. Boyd had instructed her mother to go into New Orleans and collect packages for her and Becky from two different shops.

Mary wanted to go along, because Mrs. Thatcher had given her a few days off work. She smiled to herself and excitement stirred within her as Josh drove them into town. She'd loved to look at things through the store windows, but today she had the opportunity to actually walk into a shop and look around.

When she arrived, Mary, wearing the dress and shoes Mrs. Thatcher had given her, adjusted her hat, opened the front door with her head held high, and walked right into the mercantile store. Her mother entered through the back. Mary wandered around the shop, picking out dresses and holding them up to herself in front of a mirror.

Her mother got her attention and shook her head, but Mary kept browsing.

"Take your time and look around," the shopkeeper said to Mary.

Mary's stomach fluttered as she played the role of a white woman. This was the most exciting day of her life.

Mary's mother said to the shopkeeper, "I'm here to pick up three packages for Miss Becky Boyd."

"I'm Becky," Mary lied. "I'd like to see them first."

Mary continued to browse until the shopkeeper found Becky's boxes. Just the fresh fragrance and the touch of the new fibers exhilarated her.

Her mother stood at the end of the counter. "What are you doing, child?" she whispered.

"Just looking around." Mary's fingers caressed various dresses and hats, admiring their wealth and texture.

"You trying to get me into trouble, gal?" her mother scolded in a low voice.

Mary held another pretty dress up to herself and glanced at her image in the mirror.

"That's from New York City," the shopkeeper said. He adjusted his vest and beamed at Mary. "That dress would look mighty pretty on you. It complements your hair."

"Don't touch that," her mother yelled. "Put that down."

The shopkeeper gasped, "How dare you talk like that to a white woman? What kind of master do you have? You need a good whipping."

"She's my daughter," her mother shot back.

Mary batted her eyelashes and flashed a cheerful smile. "My mother died when I was a child," she told the shopkeeper. "My maid here calls me her daughter, and I sometimes refer to her as my mother. We're very close. Not too many people can say that about their slaves."

"Oh," he said. "Still, she needs to know her place."

"You have a dress for me," Mary flirted. "I'd like to try it on."

"Try it on?" her mother growled.

The man gave her mother a disagreeable look and placed the boxes on the counter.

Mary opened the first box. "Is there a place where I can try this on?"

He pointed. "Behind the curtain. Take your time, Miss."

When Mary walked from behind the curtain wearing Becky's dress, she thought her mother would faint. Mary placed her own hat on the counter, elegantly removed Becky's hat from a box, and put it on her head. She admired herself in the mirror, feeling the prestige that came with being the daughter of a plantation owner. "These are beautiful. I love them."

This was the life Mary deserved and vowed to have one day.

"Would you like to try on the shoes?" he asked.

"No. I'm sure they'll fit."

"They look a little small," he said.

"Actually, these shoes are a bit large," she replied.

"The dress is about two inches shorter than most women wear, don't you think?" he asked.

"No," Mary said. "I actually like my dresses a little short, because I don't want them mopping the floor when I walk. Besides, why wear shoes if you can't show them off?"

"Smart. Very smart," he agreed.

Three young women entered the shop as the bell above the door rang. Two of the ladies looked to be in their early twenties. One was a blonde, the other a brunette. The third one seemed younger, about Mary's age. The shopkeeper rushed to them. "May I help you ladies?"

"We're from Philadelphia," the blonde said in a snooty tone. "Just curious about what the local women wear and where they buy their clothes."

"Look at this lovely lady." He waved a hand at Mary. "Her dress came from New York City. We have only the finest here. As far away as Paris, special ordered, of course. This may not be Philadelphia or New York City, but we can get the same merchandise."

"That is a lovely dress," the brunette said.

"You look so gorgeous in it," the youngest one said, touching Mary's shoulder.

"I live in the South now, but my parents moved here from Pennsylvania when I was a child," Mary said.

"I'd like to have a dress like this one. I promise, I'll wear it only in Philadelphia," the youngest girl said.

"We knew you must be from the East, because you

don't have that Southern drawl," the blonde said, and they all giggled.

Mary was proud of the way she spoke English, and now she had even impressed the women from back East. "Watch these Southern girls. Most of them have slaves who make their clothes. Why, I wore a dress to a ball once, and two days later I saw a copy of it, right down to the buttons."

"Thanks for telling us," the brunette said. "We won't be surprised if we see our dresses out on the town."

"Excuse me, ladies. I was just trying it on." Mary went behind the curtain, took off the dress, and placed it back into the box. "It's absolutely lovely. Thank you," she said, removing the hat as well. "I'll be back to look at other dresses sometime soon. Goodbye," she said to the shopkeeper before turning her attention back to the three women. "Ladies."

Mary's mother just stood there.

"My boxes," Mary said as she headed for the front door.

Her mother picked up the boxes, walked out the back door, and placed them into the wagon. "You just wait until I get you home, young lady."

***

At the next shop, Mary and her mother picked up things for Mrs. Boyd. Again, Mary walked through the front door while her mother entered through the back. They stood behind a customer at the counter.

"Be with you in a minute," the clerk said.

After waiting in line for an inordinate amount of time, Mary said loudly, "We're here to pick up tablecloths and linens for Mrs. Boyd."

No one outside the plantation knew Mary, with the exception of Mrs. Thatcher. The locals didn't know a black woman who looked white existed. She felt safe and secure playing her role in the shop.

"Mrs. Boyd. Oh, yes," the woman said. "Be right back."

The clerk returned shortly with one box, placed it on the counter, and then trotted back to collect the second one. "They're heavy. Do you need any help out?"

"No. The two of us can manage," Mary said.

Mary lifted one box off the counter, and her mother took the other and headed for the back door. "Since they're so heavy, can she use the front door? The wagon is just outside."

The woman smiled. "Just this once."

Once outside, Mary said, "See how I got you to walk right through the front door, Mama."

"Don't try that anymore," her mother scolded. "We both could be whipped."

***

Mary didn't go to Mrs. Thatcher's house the next day. Instead, two wagons took her and four other women to the docks to clean up Master Boyd's warehouse.

Mrs. Thatcher had told her how cargo and passengers were shipped across the Atlantic Ocean. Her parents had sailed the long voyage from England when she was a child.

White sails from two docked ships stood tall in the clear morning sky. In the distance and over the horizon, sails from another approaching vessel were visible. Excitement stirred in Mary like the breeze across the gulf as she leaped from the wagon and ran to the dock.

"Get back here, gal," the overseer said.

"I just wanted a closer look."

"We came here to work, not to go poking around," he said, unlocking a huge door and sliding it open.

When Mary and the other women walked into the dirty building, it was empty except for rats' nests, trash, and several small boxes. She had not known her master owned a warehouse at the dock area, but how would she know what he owned? Alongside the other women, Mary swept, dusted, and picked up nests, while killing any rats she came across. The men boarded up the holes in the walls and floor to prevent other rats from coming into the building.

For lunch, the overseers bought them sandwiches from a nearby restaurant. Mary ate hers while leaning against the rails of the dock, observing the dockhands moving large crates on and off the gangplanks. A man climbed up the ropes to the top of a mast, untangled lines, and then shimmied back down. She gazed at the waves and into the distant horizon and suddenly had an urge to visit faraway places.

"Lunch break is over, Mary. Let's get back to work," the overseer said. "We need to have this building cleaned today."

Mary and the other women entered the warehouse and resumed their duties. They helped the overseer load the boxes from the warehouse to the wagons, and that ended their day.

One of the dockworkers had been watching Mary. He approached her prior to their departure.

"What are you doing here?" he asked.

"What does it look like I'm doing? Working."

"Why are you working with them?" he asked.

"I'm an indentured servant," she replied.

On the way back home, they drove through the city and dropped off the boxes. Mary covered her hair and shielded her face with a scarf.

CHAPTER 5

MRS. THATCHER

MRS. THATCHER HAD expected her daughter, son-in-law, and their two children to visit last month, but they didn't show. One of the kids had gotten sick, but the letter took a long time to reach New Orleans with the news.

When Mary showed up at Mrs. Thatcher's house that Saturday morning, a man answered the front door. He stood tall with black hair and a matching, thick mustache.

"You Mary?" he asked.

Mary smiled. "Yes, you must be Mr. Edward."

"Shouldn't you be using the back door?" he said curtly.

"What?" Mary asked.

"Go around to the back door," he ordered.

Mary lowered her head and did as he instructed. She opened the back door and yelled, "Mrs. Thatcher."

"Knock, dammit," he demanded.

Mary closed the door and rapped on it loudly with her knuckles. "Mrs. Thatcher."

He opened the door. "Not so loud. Do you want to wake the kids?"

"Sorry," Mary said, grimacing. She wasn't used to anyone speaking to her in this tone of voice.

He stepped aside and allowed her to enter.

"There are dirty diapers in the bathroom. Wash them and make sure they're bright white. I don't want them looking yellow like piss," he hissed.

Mrs. Thatcher came downstairs. "Did I hear Mary?"

"Yes," the man said. "I gave her a job, washing the baby's diapers."

"Hello, Mrs. Thatcher," Mary yelled from the bathroom.

"I asked you to keep the damn noise down," he warned.

"Both kids are already awake, Edward," Mrs. Thatcher said.

"You need to get rid of that slave living upstairs," Edward complained. "She's good for nothing. Not even worth selling. Why not just turn her out to pasture?"

"Oh, Edward. How will she survive?"

"Who cares? Get rid of her," he urged.

"She was my children's maid. She practically raised them, like a mother."

"She's a slave. That was her duty," he snapped.

"She doesn't eat much. Most of the time, I don't even know she's here."

"Exactly my point," Mr. Edward said. "This place needs cleaning. The dirt on the windowsills is so thick I can write my name in it."

Mary took the wash outside, giving Mrs. Thatcher and her son-in-law privacy.

Most of the diapers were too ripe to touch. Some contained urine and others held dried feces. How many days had they been carrying these stinky things around? Mary rinsed out the feces and had a pot of hot water heating on the stove. She first washed the diapers in cold water in a foot tub and then placed them into a #3 tub, where she used a rubbing board to wash them in warm water. She hung them on the clothesline to dry and only hoped the sun would bleach them.

When Mrs. Thatcher walked to the wash station in the backyard, Edward stood behind her. "I'll have my driver take you home, Mary."

"You sure?" Mary asked.

"Are you questioning her order?" Mr. Edward demanded.

Mary cringed. She didn't like Mr. Edward, and he frightened her. "No, sir."

***

Three days later, Mrs. Thatcher sent her driver to fetch Mary. John was about forty years old and thin, with a beard. He rode up to her house in his wagon that morning and yelled, "Mary."

Mary opened the door and peeked out. "Yes, John?"

"Mrs. Thatcher wants you to work today if you're not already doing something for Master Boyd."

"No," Mary said. "I don't have a thing to do."

She walked out and climbed into his wagon.

As John drove off, she asked, "How long have you been working for Mrs. Thatcher?"

"Years," John said. "Most of the time I just sit around idle, waiting to drive her places."

"Her son-in-law is mean to me," Mary commented.

"He's mean to all of us," John said. "Thinks he's above us. Said I didn't know how to drive a wagon, because I hit too many bumps. Tried to get Mrs. Thatcher to sell me and buy herself a new driver."

"I think that's why she sent me home the last time I was there—because of the way he treated me," Mary said.

"He has been on her back about getting rid of Hattie May too."

"I heard," Mary said.

"I don't think Mrs. Thatcher likes him either."

"I'll keep clear of him," Mary said.

"With him being in the house all day, I doubt if that's possible. He wants you to clean the place from top to bottom." John exited off the main road and onto Mrs. Thatcher's long driveway. He drove the wagon behind the house and stopped.

Mary jumped down. "You'll have to take me home, because Josh doesn't know I'm here."

"If I go out that way, I'll let him know. If I can't find him, Mrs. Thatcher will call me when you're ready to leave."

"If you see Josh, tell him to pick me up as early as possible."

John chuckled. "Will do."

Mary walked to the back door and knocked. No one answered, so she opened the door and quietly called, "Mrs. Thatcher."

Mrs. Thatcher's daughter came to the door. "Hello, Mary. My name is Diane. I didn't get a chance to meet you the last time you were here. My, my, you're as beautiful as Mother said."

"Thank you. That's always nice to hear."

Diane leaned in closer and whispered, "Ever thought about moving East?"

Mrs. Thatcher's daughter was nice, just like her mother.

"It has crossed my mind a few times. There's nothing for me here."

"Get my address from Mother and look me up if you do."

"I will. Thank you."

Mr. Edward entered the room then. "Mary, there are some more diapers to wash today, and we need you to mop the floors and wash the lower windows." Then he turned his attention to his wife. "I've been on your mother about getting rid of that slave living upstairs."

Diane said, "Edward, she has no place to go. She'd starve if we turned her away from here."

Mary took the laundry outside while Diane had a private discussion with her husband about how Mrs. Thatcher should manage her slaves. Mary knew Mrs. Thatcher would never turn Hattie May out to die on the streets or sell and replace John.

After Mary washed the clothes, dusted, mopped, washed windows, and replaced the bed linens, Mrs. Thatcher's daughter made them sandwiches for lunch. Mary even had playtime with the children—two boys, ages one and three.

Josh picked her up early that evening. "Never seen you looking so tired after a day at Mrs. Thatcher's house," he commented.

"Her daughter is here with her family. I have another long day tomorrow. They're working me to death."

When Mary got home, she ate and collapsed on her bed.

***

Josh woke Mary up early the next morning, pounding on the front door. "Mary," he yelled.

She jumped out of bed, dressed, and rushed out to the wagon.

"Unlike you to sleep late," he said, driving off.

"Sorry, Josh," she replied, yawning.

"How do you like Mrs. Thatcher's folks?"

"Her daughter is nice. I love the kids, but her husband

is the worst of the evil plantation owners. He treats me like dirt."

Mary never thought she'd see the day she would hate going to Mrs. Thatcher's house.

"Just stay out of his way," he said.

"That's hard to do when every time I turn around he's standing there, watching me as if he's waiting for me to do something wrong."

"Everything will settle back to normal once they're gone."

"They'll be here for another three weeks."

When Mary arrived at Mrs. Thatcher's house, her first duty for the day was feeding the kids, then washing the diapers again. She took the large living room rugs outside and beat out the dirt with a stick, cooked, and cleaned up the kitchen. John washed the upstairs windows from a ladder while Mary cleaned the inside. She dusted and changed the linens on the other four beds, although no one had slept in them.

***

Another week had passed, and Mary avoided Mr. Edward as much as possible. Mrs. Thatcher and her daughter went into New Orleans for a day of shopping, leaving the children with Mary.

When Mary played with the kids, Mr. Edward was there. She took the baby and the three-year-old outside, and he followed, watching her every move. Mary took the kids into the kitchen, prepared lunch, and fed them while Edward stood watch. It was difficult to get them to take a nap, because he was there interfering. Finally, both children fell asleep.

She was washing dishes when she turned around and found Mr. Edward leaning against the doorframe with his arms folded across his chest, watching her.

She hated him but hinted a smile. "I finally got the kids to sleep."

He didn't reply.

"Mrs. Thatcher said they're having lunch in town today."

Still no response.

She turned and gazed at him again, and then continued washing the dishes.

"How can someone like you turn out to be such a lustful wench?"

Her heart thumped in her chest. Quickly turning, she asked, "What did you say?"

"You heard me, wench. Get upstairs and take off your clothes."

Mary had a dishcloth in one hand and silverware in the other.

She'd seen eyes like his. A dim light of hateful lust stirred in them.

His evil eyes followed hers to the drawer that housed the kitchen knives. He stepped closer, blocking the distance between her and the knives.

"You better not touch me, you bastard."

"Harsh words from a lady."

Mary dropped the dishcloth, threw the handful of silverware into Mr. Edward's face, and tried to duck past him. He grabbed her hands, forced them behind her back, and led her into the living room. Mary screamed. He was so strong, and she felt so weak and helpless. Her only chance was to get him between the legs, so she tried desperately to free her hands but couldn't break from his stout hold. She maneuvered her head around, bit his shoulder, and drew blood. He let go, then slapped her with a weighty backhanded swing.

She exclaimed in dismay, "You better leave me alone."

Blood ran down the side of Mary's mouth as she wiped it with the back of her hand. Mr. Edward straddled her, reached down, and ripped off the upper part of her dress. Mary dove for his private parts, but he lurched back. She covered her bare breasts with her arms and cried out, "Don't hurt me."

Mary tried to stand, but he pushed her back to the floor. This time he ripped off the lower half of her dress, and she lay naked on the living room floor, sobbing.

He unbuckled his belt, unbuttoned his pants, and let them fall around his ankles. When she tried to stand again, he slapped her back to the floor.

"Looks like we're going to have to do this here," he said.

Mr. Edward hated Mary, detested her. Why was he doing this? She tried kicking him in the groin, but her feet couldn't reach. Grabbing her ankles, he spread her legs and fell on top of her, holding her hands against the floor. This couldn't be happening to her. Not in Mrs. Thatcher's house. Mary screamed for the driver, the maid, anybody. Then she saw two sets of feet, then legs.

"Edward," Diane yelled.

"Get him off me," Mary screamed. "Please don't let him rape me."

Mr. Edward rolled off Mary, his face as white as the paint on the house. Embarrassed at his actions and his state of undress, he turned over on the floor and tried to hide himself.

Mary grabbed the torn pieces of her dress and covered herself, sobbing uncontrollably. This was the second time a man had tried to rape her. She hated the South and being black.

Shock covered the women's faces.

"What?" Diane yelled.

By this time, Mr. Edward had wiggled into his pants and buttoned them up.

A smear of crimson, mixed with tears, rolled down Mary's chin.

Mr. Edward left the living room while the two women just stood there, still in utter shock.

"I want to go home," Mary whimpered, shaking like a leaf in the wind.

Finally, Mrs. Thatcher said, barely above a whisper, "I'll get you a dress, Mary."

When Mrs. Thatcher returned with the dress, Mary was sitting on the floor, rocking back and forth. Using the kitchen counter to support herself, she stood on shaky legs and donned the dress. *Will Mrs. Thatcher blame me—think it was my fault and hate me?*

Mary cried out, "Please let me go home, Mrs. Thatcher."

"I'll get John to drive you, dear," Mrs. Thatcher said.

Diane still stood frozen like a statue.

When Mary left, the house was deathly quiet. She cried all the way home, and John didn't ask any questions—not why she was crying, why she was wearing a different dress, or how she got a busted lip. Slaves never interfered with what white folks did to other slaves.

When her parents arrived home, she told them what had happened.

"Go to Master Boyd. Tell him you don't want to go to Mrs. Thatcher's house as long as her son-in-law is there," her mother said.

"I'll tell him Sunday," Mary agreed.

CHAPTER 6

DINNER DATE

THE NEXT SUNDAY morning, Master Boyd sent Josh to Mary's house with boxes from a local New Orleans shop.

She opened the packages one by one and found the most beautiful green dress, a matching hat, and new shoes. Mary had orders to be ready by six o'clock that evening, because Master Boyd was taking her into town to have supper with his friend. She became so ecstatic, she couldn't catch her breath.

Mary patted her chest. "Mama, I think I'm going to faint. I feel … lightheaded."

Mary had just turned seventeen, and she was sure Master Boyd had found her a husband. She hoped it was Mr. Charles. He was so handsome.

"Why does Master Boyd want you to go into town with him, Mary?" her mother asked.

"He has found me a husband, I'm sure. This is the happiest day of my life, Mama."

"A husband?" Walter asked. "It would be funny if it wasn't so silly."

Mary took a deep breath and let it out slowly. "To meet his friend. I just know it's Mr. Charles. The one who visits the big house on Saturdays. He has had his eye on me for quite some time now."

"Are you out of your mind, girl?" Walter said. "No white man is going to marry you."

Ignoring him, Mary held the dress up to herself and twirled around in front of her family. "Just look at this dress." She admired herself in the mirror. "He sent me this perfume too." She dabbed some on her mother's arm. "Doesn't it smell wonderful? And look at this hat," Mary said, placing it on her head like a crown. She turned to her mother like a child who had just received something special in her life. "Pin up my hair, Mama, as Becky wears hers."

"Tell him you don't want to go," her mother advised.

Mary pouted. "He told me to come. I can't say no."

"Tell him you're sick and can't make the trip. He's up to no good. I know that man. He's the devil himself. Do you think I volunteered to lay with him, child? He had me move into the big house so he could have me when he wanted. Sure, he be nice to you, because he's expecting something."

"I'm just going to supper with him and his friend, Mama," Mary giggled. "To a restaurant."

Mary was so excited, she'd washed her hair, taken a bath, and by four that afternoon was dressed like a princess, which was exactly the way she felt. She had totally forgotten about Mr. Edward ... and the mark on her lip was barely visible. Her mother had brushed and pinned up her hair, and when Mary saw herself in the mirror, she looked ravishing.

Josh showed up in a carriage rather than the wagon.

Mary's heart was thumping in her chest like a drum, and she couldn't contain it. This was her first time off the plantation as a white woman. Master Boyd had her dressed elegantly, like a lady—not in rags like a slave.

Her master sat in the back of the carriage. Mary hesitated, not knowing whether to sit in the front with Josh or in the back with Master Boyd.

"Sit back here with me, my dear. I have a friend I'd like you to meet, Mary. Be nice to him," Master Boyd said.

She sat in the back of the carriage with him, her mind whirring like a dustbowl. Master Boyd spoke not another word to her during the entire trip, and Mary was too afraid to utter a sound. She felt disappointed, because he hadn't complimented her concerning how pretty she looked.

When they arrived at a hotel, Master Boyd stepped down from the carriage. Like a perfect gentleman, he took Mary's hand in his and helped her to the ground. She gathered up her dress and stepped down with her hand in his. It was the first and only time she remembered him touching her. He always dressed nicely but had an old man's smell about him. Josh remained outside with the carriage while Mary and Master Boyd walked through the front door of the hotel and up to the third floor. Her dream was coming true.

Master Boyd knocked on the door of room 311. When it opened, Mary was disappointed. Charles wasn't on the other side of the door, but an old, haggard-looking man with a cigar wedged in the corner of his mouth. She hoped they didn't see the disappointment in her eyes.

The man was older than Master Boyd and smaller in stature. He had thinning hair and rotten front teeth. Although he was dressed rather nicely, he stank worse than the slaves did. A long gray beard hung down on his chest, and his gray eyes reminded her of a dead rabbit's she'd found floating in the creek one day.

The room was average, nothing special, she noted as she looked around. The bedspread had a green floral print with a headboard for storing things. A layer of books lined the center, and a vase of magnolia flowers was perched on top. A dining table stood in the center of the small, cramped room. Draped over it was a white tablecloth with white dishes and real silverware. A bottle of whiskey and three glasses stood on the table.

Another small table and two chairs were wedged between the chifforobe and the opposite wall. There was an oil lamp on the table along with a metal statue of an elephant.

"Mary, this is Mr. Amos from Texas. I promised him some company tonight. You don't mind keeping company with him after supper, do you?"

"After supper?" she asked. Mary didn't understand what Master Boyd meant. Not wanting to seem stupid, she just dropped the subject. However, she did mind conversing with a dirty old man she couldn't stand.

"We're having dinner here in Mr. Amos's room," Master Boyd went on. "I promise you'll love the food."

"You're quite a lovely little thing," Mr. Amos said. He pulled out her chair, and she sat at the side of the table between them.

She was hoping someone else was going to show up, but the table had only three place settings. "How about some whiskey?" Mr. Amos asked.

"A tall glass for me," Master Boyd said. "A glass for Mary too."

Amos poured three glasses of whiskey. The glass sat before Mary, but she didn't touch it.

"I just bought three huge bucks from a farm in Texas," Mr. Amos chuckled. Pulling the cigar from his mouth, he dropped it into an ashtray. "This one owner has a whole breed of giants. Cost me twelve hundred apiece. Worth every penny."

"My daughter, Becky, has been trying to get me to sell off some of my stock. I do have more than I need. Each wench brings me an average of ten babies."

"I'm glad I planted lots of cotton this year," Mr. Amos continued. "The price in Europe has gone up."

"I'm getting rid of most of my cows next year," Master Boyd added. "I'll make more in crops and won't have to worry about that much hay during the winter months."

"What about your horses?" Mr. Amos asked.

"I have thirty-three thoroughbreds left. I'm not raising any more horses after I sell those," Master Boyd said. "I'm planting more cotton."

Mr. Amos removed a cigar from his inside pocket and handed it to Master Boyd. "Maybe you should keep your extra slaves."

Master Boyd accepted the cigar and placed it in his mouth while Mr. Amos lit it with a match. He took a powerful draw, and smoke escaped his mouth as he spoke. "No. I'll just work the remaining ones harder. I have lots of young boys who'll be old enough to pick cotton in a couple of years."

The men continued their conversation about plantation business and the price of slaves—something Mary knew nothing about and didn't want to hear. They acted as if she wasn't there at all, so she picked up the glass in front of her and took a gulp of whiskey. It burned her throat, eyes, and nose. She frantically coughed and dropped her glass, spilling the remainder of the drink in her lap and on the table. Gasping for air, she placed her hands over her mouth and choked out, "I'm sorry." Her eyes welled up and tears spilled down her cheeks. She wiped her face with both hands, but the tears kept coming. *Why would someone drink something that tastes so awful?*

Mr. Amos patted her hand and then squeezed it.

Mary cringed.

There was a knock at the door. Mr. Amos walked over with an awkward gait, opened it, and stepped aside. "Come on in. We're starving."

A server entered, pushing a cart. He smiled. "Here you are, folks. My, don't this smell delicious?"

He placed a plate of jambalaya before each of them, as well as a large bowl of crawfish to share. He left a pitcher of lemonade in the center of the table with hot rolls and glasses.

"Will there be anything else? Something from the bar? Wine?"

"No. We have our own whiskey," Mr. Amos said.

Mary was glad when dinner arrived. She could eat and not sit there looking stupid. Mrs. Thatcher had taught her table etiquette, but she was still nervous about the setting just the same. She picked up her fork, dug in, and remained silent.

"Enjoying your meal, Mary?" Mr. Amos asked.

"Yes," she replied. "It's delicious."

"I just love Creole food," Master Boyd interjected.

If her master was trying to get her hitched, she preferred a younger, better-looking man—not an old, balding man with liver spots all over his hands and face.

After dinner, the room got rather stuffy, considering body odor, cigar smoke, and the stench of whiskey.

"How about trying another glass of whiskey, Mary?" Mr. Amos asked.

"No, thank you, sir."

"Why don't we mix it," Master Boyd said, pouring whiskey into a glass of lemonade.

She looked at her master.

"Go on," he urged.

"I don't want any more," Mary protested.

"It's all right," Mr. Amos said, patting her hand. "She doesn't like it. It takes some getting used to. I remember my first drink. We don't need whiskey to help us get acquainted, do we, my dear?"

After his meal, Master Boyd burped. "I'll have another drink of whiskey and be off."

He poured a fourth of a glass, gulped it down, and stood. "Goodnight. I'll send Josh for you in the morning, Mary."

Mary jumped to her feet and rushed to Master Boyd's side, mind whirling. "You can't leave me here with a man I don't know."

"I'll take it from here," Mr. Amos said.

Master Boyd opened the door and stepped into the hallway. "I can, and I will. Do what he tells you. Comfort him tonight."

Now Mary knew why she was there. Her entire world came crashing down around her. Her mother and Walter were right. Master Boyd was using her. He expected her to sleep with his friend.

"Goodnight, Amos," Master Boyd said. Stepping into the hallway, he closed the door behind him.

Mary didn't cry from disappointment, although she felt as if she would. She slowly turned and gazed at the old, pathetic man. Feeling like a complete fool and shaking her head wildly, she said, "I will not."

He smiled. "You want that drink now?"

"I will not sleep with you or any man unless I choose to."

Master Boyd is my real father. How could he do this to me? No father would do such a thing to his own flesh and blood.

"Look. You're a slave. You do what a white man tells you to do." He took a gulp of his drink and gave her a sullen look. The lines deepened across his wrinkled forehead. "I'm telling you to take your clothes off and come to bed with me." He removed his tie.

She held her stomach, waiting for it to rupture, but it didn't come. "No. I will not do anything of the sort." Tears rolled down her cheeks. She rushed to the door, wanting to catch Master Boyd before he and Josh left.

Mr. Amos grabbed her arm. "You've been spoiled, little girl."

She forced her arm from his grip. "I'd rather die than let you touch me, you old, dirty man. You stink. Don't you ever bathe?"

He slapped her face. "Get on that bed and take off your clothes," he demanded, eyes dark and angry.

When she didn't move, he tackled her onto the bed. He was all over her. She clawed his genitals, digging her fingers into him.

Grabbing his private parts with his hands, he rolled over and cried, "You little wench."

She dashed for the door, but he jumped on her back and brought her down. She rolled over and elbowed him in the mouth.

He let go and said, "Get back here."

Grabbing her again, he tried to pin her hands to the floor, but she bit him on his neck, leaving a foul taste in her mouth.

He slapped her again.

She punched him in the mouth, climbed to her feet, and kicked him between his legs.

He went down on the floor like a ragdoll.

Rushing to the door, she threw it open and ran down the stairs and through the lobby.

The man behind the desk called after her as she rushed out, "Miss, is there a problem?"

Mary didn't stop or turn around. Master Boyd and Josh had left in the carriage, so she frantically ran down the street and blended into the nighttime crowd.

Frightened to death, she roamed the streets. She'd never been out in the world all by herself, and the crowd terrified her. She crossed her arms, fingernails digging into her flesh. People dined in restaurants and laughed in nightclubs where music flowed into the streets. There were nice-looking people, strange-looking people, and simple-looking people.

Mary hated her father for presenting her as a wench.

She wanted to kill him as she'd killed Joe Joe. How dare he treat her like an animal? She wanted him to love her, to be kind and gentle to her as a father should. Her heart felt heavy, burdened with disappointment. She was only a slave to him.

Her mother and Walter had tried to tell her how things were, but she had refused to accept the facts. Mary was actually dumb enough to think she was different, that she had a better chance in life because of her looks. She had to face the truth. She was just a fair-skinned girl who got a break from being a slave. But that was about to change.

Finding herself walking on the shady side of town, she turned around and headed back in the direction of the hotel. With no money and no way home, she asked a stranger where the stage depot was. Josh had said it stayed open all night. However, when she arrived, it had closed for the evening. She read the coach schedule on the window.

"Hello, young lady. Leaving town?" A nicely dressed man who smelled good approached her. He was the tallest man she'd ever seen.

"In a few days."

"Where are you going?" he asked.

"Do you work here?"

"No."

"Then you can't help me."

He smiled. "I wouldn't say that. Where are you trying to go?"

"New York City. I want to join the theater."

"You have the looks for it. Bet you can make it in show business."

"You've been to New York?"

"Once. Hated it. Too crowded. Too busy."

She looked into his eyes, but they were vacant. "I understand there are lots of opportunities there."

"Some make it; most don't."

"I'll remember that … goodnight." She started to walk away.

"Hey," he yelled at her back. "Can I buy you dinner?"

"No," she said over her shoulder and continued walking.

There was something evil about the man—most men, as she was discovering.

She found a nightclub and walked in.

"Are you alone?" the man at the door asked.

"Yes."

"Sorry, we don't allow lone women in here."

"She's with me."

Mary turned and saw a young man standing behind her.

"Let's find a table," he said.

They couldn't find a vacant table, so they stood against the wall.

"What'll you have?"

"Nothing," she said.

"A glass of wine, perhaps?"

"No. I just want to talk."

"What's your name?"

"Mary."

"Mary what?"

"Isn't Mary enough?" *I don't even have a last name.*

"All right, Mary. Let's talk. How old are you?"

"You first."

"I'm twenty-four. I'm a sailor. Ever been to the docks?"

"Yes."

"I haven't sailed the world yet, but I'm working on it. What about you?"

"I'm thinking about going to school back East, New York City to be exact."

"I've been there. Great place to visit, but I wouldn't live there."

"Why not?"

"It's too crowded. Everything is too expensive, and they let black people walk around free."

"You were born in the South?"

"Mississippi. Lost my Southern accent."

"Excuse me. I need to go out back."

"There's a lantern on the door," he said.

Mary went out the back door, but rather than going to the outhouse, she continued walking. Finding an empty bench, she took a seat.

Several well-dressed men stopped and asked her to dinner, but she refused. One man with luxurious black hair, graying at the temples, sat on a bench and talked with her.

"Why does such a beautiful young lady like yourself look so sad?" he asked. His voice was warm and friendly.

"I had a shocking experience tonight with a man," she admitted.

He gasped, "He didn't hurt you, did he?"

"No, I ran away. But I can still smell the stench of him. And now I have no money and no way home."

"Where's your purse?"

"He has it."

"Want me to find a peace officer?"

"No. There was only five dollars in it."

"Do you have a friend you can spend the night with?"

"No. I don't know anyone here."

"I'll have my driver take you home, young lady."

"No. I don't want to be a bother." Truthfully, she didn't want him to see where she lived.

"Let's find a table in a restaurant."

"I've already had supper … dinner."

"Then watch me eat. There's a nice place about two blocks from here. I eat there each time I visit New Orleans." He stood. "My name is Jeff."

"Mary."

She trailed along with him like a lost child. They walked in silence for a while.

"This is the place. Antoine's. Have you ever eaten here?"

"No," she answered.

He opened the door and allowed her to enter first.

She stepped inside, eyes searching for an empty table.

A young man approached them with menus. "Table for two?"

"Yes," he said.

"This way," the young man said.

The place was crowded. Plain white tablecloths were on every table, with a burning candle enclosed in a glass in each center.

The waiter led them to a table next to a window. "How about this?"

"Fine with me," she said.

"We'll take it," he agreed.

"You're not from here?" she asked.

"New York City. I'm in the shipping business and make trips to most ports in this country and to the Caribbean. Own my own company."

"What do you ship?" she asked.

"You name it. Cotton, tobacco, slaves."

She shivered. "Slaves?"

He smiled. "If there's a demand, I deliver."

"Don't you feel guilty about uprooting people from their home, family, and country for money and treating them like animals?"

He chuckled. "They are animals."

"They are human beings, just like you and me."

He read his menu. "I can see you're one of those sympathizers. Human rights and all that junk. You sure you don't want anything?"

She thought he was a kind and gentle man, but she'd been disappointed once already tonight.

The waiter returned. "Y'all ready to order?"

Jeff placed his order and closed the menu.

"And for the lady?" the waiter asked.

"Lemonade," she said and then continued. "This country has abolished the slave trade. It's people like you who are breaking the law."

"The law is in writing, but not enforced, my dear."

She dropped the slave subject and started talking about other things. She wanted to know more about New York City and his visits to other ports.

"What business do you have in the Caribbean?"

"I ship sugarcane from the Caribbean."

"What's the Caribbean like?"

"There are many slaves to do the work there. Not many places to live or socialize like here in America."

"Then why go there?"

"To take care of business," he said.

"Don't you pay someone to do that for you?"

"Yes, but even the help needs checking up on every now and then."

Excitement stirred in her voice. "Have you ever been to Europe?"

"A few times. I don't like long voyages. On my second trip, I spent two months in Europe. I arrived in England and took a coach to different countries. Most of them are small. Not large like America."

"I'd like to visit Europe someday."

His dinner arrived.

She stood. "Thanks for the lemonade."

"I thought you were going to watch me eat," he said.

She had no place to go, so she took her seat.

As he ate, they had a little conversation.

Shortly after, he dabbed the corners of his mouth on a napkin and dropped it on the side of his plate. "Well," he concluded, "that was a fine meal. Would you like to come to my room? It's not far from here."

"No. I don't visit men's rooms."

"You don't look like the type. How do you plan to get back home?"

"A friend of mine will be in town tomorrow morning. I can ride back with him."

"Do you live on a plantation?"

"Yes," she replied honestly.

"Aren't your folks worried about you?"

"I suppose so."

"Don't you have slaves on your plantation?"

"Many. They do all the work."

"Who bought them?"

"My father."

"You don't agree with him buying slaves?"

"No. If I had my way, I'd free them all. Pay them to work and educate them so they could become independent, just like the ones back East."

"Good for you. You can sit in my room for tonight. I'll be a perfect gentleman."

"Just for a while," she agreed.

"Good. I have a bottle of red wine just waiting to breathe a little air."

"I don't drink."

"You smell of whiskey."

"This man I was having dinner with gave me a glass. I didn't like the taste, and I spilled it all over my dress."

He dropped some bills on the table, and they walked out together.

She noticed crowds of people on the streets now, and numerous carriages were waiting around corners for their owners to return.

When Mary and Jeff walked into his hotel, everyone in the lobby turned and stared at them. His room was on the first floor. He pulled a key from his pocket and opened the door. The room was nicer than Mr. Amos's had been. The chifforobe door stood open. It contained many fine clothes, and two pairs of shoes sat on the floor beneath his wardrobe. He removed his jacket and laid it on the bed. As he'd mentioned, a bottle of wine sat on a table with two chairs. He uncorked it and poured two glasses.

"Have a seat." He pulled back one of the chairs at the table, and she sat. Jeff took the chair across from her, swirled the wine around in his glass, and sniffed it.

"Taste it. Straight from Italy," he said, taking a sip.

"No, thanks."

"Just one glass."

She didn't see a wedding ring. "You never talked about a family."

"I have a boring wife and two out-of-control teenage boys. They're exactly why I travel most of the time."

"Why don't you just get a divorce?"

"It's not financially reasonable. So, most of the time, I just pretend they don't exist."

"I don't think I could live with a man if I were unhappy with him."

"It was a mistake, and I have to live with it. I do court other women. I can be very generous to my lady friends."

"I don't have a need for anything."

"I doubt that." He scooted his chair in closer, then placed a hand on hers. "Drink up."

"Are you trying to get me drunk?"

"No. I just want you to enjoy yourself. How old are you?"

"Seventeen."

"Oh. I thought you were older."

"No. I'm still considered a child, so don't get any ideas." He stood. "Goodnight, my dear."

She blurted out, "What if I'm black, the daughter of a slave? What would you say then?"

A devious smile spread across his face. "I would force you to participate in whatever I want, and no matter how old you are, no one—absolutely no one—would care."

She hated him, but she knew what he said was true. He was worse than Master Boyd and Joe Joe all in one. "You've assaulted women in the past, haven't you?"

Her mother ran outside. "Stop hurting my child, please."

"What did she do?" Walter asked.

After the beating, they untied Mary's hands and left her on the ground. Walter picked her up, carried her inside the house, and laid her on their bed.

Her mother cut the bloody dress from Mary's back as her daughter wept in pain. "Bring me some butter," she said to her son. Her mother spread butter on the wounds as Mary continued to bawl hysterically.

Walter asked, "Why did he have you whipped, Mary? What did you do?"

There was silence in the room as Mary told the story as it had unfolded that night.

"That bastard," Walter said when she'd finished. "I'd like to kill him. I'm a man, and I can't do anything to safeguard my own women."

"I hate him, Mama. I hate him. He treated me like …" Mary buried her head into the bed and sobbed louder.

Her mother shivered. "He's going to try it again. I thought you were safe, protected."

"Then he'll have to beat me again and again. I won't do it. I just won't do it," Mary promised. She knew she had to leave the plantation and the South soon.

"You still have those dresses Mrs. Thatcher gave you?" Walter asked. "Will she give you enough money for a stage ticket East?"

"I have some money," she admitted. "Mrs. Thatcher gives me some, once a month. It's hidden."

"Get out of the South, child," her mother said. "No one knows who you are. You can take a stage, and no one will be the wiser."

"She'll need some spending money until she can find a job," Walter said to his wife.

"I'll leave in a couple of weeks," Mary replied. "You know we'll never see each other again?"

Her mother wept. "We want you safe, honey."

"I need to find out how much a stage ticket costs. It might be faster to sail to New York City."

"Don't tell anyone," her mother insisted.

"Who am I going to tell? I don't have any friends."

"You'd better keep your mouth shut, gal," Walter said. "We could all be whipped or hanged if what we're planning gets out."

Chapter 7

Where Is Mr.Edward?

A WEEK LATER, John drove up to Mary's front door. "Mary," he yelled. "You in there?"

She opened the door and stepped out on the front porch barefoot. "Yes, John."

"Mrs. Thatcher wants you at her house."

Mary was reluctant to go but couldn't refuse. "Are her daughter and her husband still there?"

"No," John assured her. "They left a few days ago. Mrs. Diane and her husband weren't on good terms."

"Let me get my shoes," Mary said.

Still, Mary felt afraid. Would Mrs. Thatcher blame her for the incident with Mr. Edward?

John and Mary rode in silence.

Mary was shaking in fear when she stepped down from the wagon. Slowly she walked to the back door, then knocked. "Mrs. Thatcher," she called in a weak voice. "You in there?"

"Yes. Come on in, dear," the old woman said from the kitchen. "You don't have to use the back door."

Sheepishly, Mary entered.

The woman was eating toast and jelly with a cup of steaming tea at her side. "My daughter brought me lots of romance novels from back East, and I'm eager to have you read them to me."

"I'd love to, Mrs. Thatcher. Any cleaning need to be done?"

"No," she said. "All that cleaning stuff was my son-in-law's idea. I just want you to read to me today."

"Are you angry at me?" Mary asked.

"Whatever for?" Mrs. Thatcher shoved a book across the table to Mary.

For a brief moment, Mary thought, *If I ever make it to New York City, I'm going to find Mr. Edward and teach him a lesson.*

Mary informed Mrs. Thatcher of what Master Boyd had planned for her with his friend at the hotel in New Orleans. The old woman was appalled. "You need to leave the South, Mary. Why don't we go into town today? I'm going to take you shopping. We can have lunch at a nice restaurant. Let's take in a play, then dinner. I promise you'll love it."

Mary became so excited she almost peed on herself. "Do you really mean it, Mrs. Thatcher?"

John picked them up at the front door. Mary sat in the back of the carriage with the mistress and chatted. She couldn't withhold her joy and enthusiasm.

First, they ate lunch at the same restaurant Jeff had taken her to a few nights prior. Admirers of Mary stopped at their table.

"Mrs. Thatcher, who's this lovely lady?" a gentleman asked.

"This is my niece, Mary, from back East," the woman said.

The man took Mary's hand in his and kissed it. "May I call on you sometime, my dear?"

"Sorry," Mary said, "but I'm to be married soon."

As they strolled down the streets of New Orleans, men stared and approached Mary, and she loved the attention.

Then they stopped at the mercantile Mary had visited to try on Becky's dress. She was surprised the shopkeeper still remembered her. Mrs. Thatcher purchased two nice dresses for her. They wandered the streets some more and ended up at the theater, where they watched a live show.

This would be Mary's turning point in life. She would settle for nothing less than living free—as a white woman, she promised herself.

Mary didn't arrive home until eleven o'clock that night. Mrs. Thatcher had told her she didn't have to come in the next day, but Mary insisted. She didn't want to be apart from the lady, her friend and mentor, who had been so kind and made her happy.

***

A few days later, Mary rode in the wagon with Josh and two boys leading a string of six horses to another plantation. She wanted to get away from home, and this trip would take them straight through New Orleans. Not wanting to look like a slave, but the daughter of a master, she wore a dress Mrs. Thatcher had given her, and on top of her pinned-up hair, a hat perched delicately on her head. She loved the trip through town and asked Josh to drive slowly. The environment excited her. She watched women shopping, running errands, eating lunch at restaurants, or walking about with their beaus on their arms. Mary wanted that life—demanded it.

As the slaves delivered the horses, a young man rode over on a bay mare with four white socks.

"I've never seen you around. You from here?" he asked, stepping off his horse.

He was in his early twenties with red hair and green eyes, a handsome face, but a little short—about her height.

"No. Just visiting," Mary said. "I'm from New York City."

"I've never been out of Louisiana. That's a nice string of horses. Do you ride?"

She flirted, "Never been on a horse."

"Most people from back East don't know how to ride. I'd love to teach you."

"No, thanks. I'm a city girl. New York City has operas, theaters, and all sorts of attractions. There are shops there that sell nothing but ladies' dresses. That's what I like, not smelly horses."

Not one to give up, he then said, "May I call on you sometime?"

"No. I'm engaged, and my fiancé is pretty jealous."

"I don't blame him," the man said.

As the slaves approached the wagon, Mary said, "Sorry, but I must be going."

"Why are you traveling with them," he hinted with his head.

"I got pretty bored just sitting around the plantation all day. The drive is nice."

"Will you be at the Magnolia Ball?" the young man asked.

"No. We'll be leaving town before then."

"Too bad," he said.

But he had made her feel good inside—beautiful, in fact—and had given her a sense of belonging to a better class.

The two boys sat on the back of the wagon. After they passed through town again, Mary accompanied the youngest, with her feet dangling off the back, as they rode homeward. It felt good to have someone her age to talk with.

"Hello, Mary," he said. "My name is Cyris."

"I remember you, but I never knew your name. You delivered food to our house a few times."

"That's right," he said.

"They don't say nice things about me, do they?" Mary asked.

"I just know that your family lives in a house and likes to be left alone."

"The women don't like me," she pressed. "I've heard some of the remarks they make about me and my family."

"They're just jealous," he said.

"Because I don't work in the fields ..."

"That too. I'm not like them. I don't have anything against you or your family. I just want to get to know you. I see you sitting in your yard a lot. Everyone needs a friend."

"What do you do, Cyris, other than work the fields?"

"Not much to do but rest. I'd like to learn how to draw, but I got no paper."

I could bring him some paper, but the overseers would whip him if they caught him with it.

"I just turned seventeen, how about you?" Mary asked.

"Seventeen, soon to be eighteen in a few months," Cyris said. "If I see you outside, is it all right if I come over and talk with you? Sunday is the only time I can visit."

"Sure. I'd love to have someone to talk to."

All the slaves knew that Master Boyd had had Mary whipped, but no one knew why. She knew that one day Cyris would ask her, but not today. They had just become acquainted.

The wagon pulled up to the slave quarters. Mary jumped off the back and headed home.

"See you next Sunday, Mary."

She turned and waved. "Bye, Cyris."

CHAPTER 8

MR.CHARLES

CHARLES WAS A good-looking, twenty-five-year-old man. His family owned a farm a few miles away, though not nearly as large as Master Boyd's plantation. He had been ogling Mary for quite some time, and she liked it. Charles was about six feet tall with auburn hair and a handsome smile. His family visited Master Boyd's plantation about twice a month for Saturday dinner. His mother and sister were always with him. One afternoon, while Mary was sitting under a tree in the front of her house, Charles stopped his carriage out of earshot of his relatives and walked toward her. Her heart started palpitating out of control.

"Hello, Mary. I'm Charles. I've admired you from a distance for many weeks."

She smiled and blushed. "I know your name, sir."

"Could you meet me at the creek behind your house a week from tomorrow? I'd like to talk to you in private."

"What time?" Mary asked.

"After dinner, about three o'clock. Would that time work for you?"

"Sure. See you then."

Mary's mother walked outside after Charles had left. "What did he want?"

"He wants to talk to me, get to know me."

"Are you out of your mind? He's looking for only one thing, and it's between your legs, girl. I forbid you to see him alone. Is that clear?"

"Yes, Mama," Mary said, even though she intended to ignore her mother. This was her chance to marry and live a normal life as a white woman. She wouldn't tell a soul—not even Mrs. Thatcher would know about Charles.

***

Mary's week went by slowly. Days got longer. Even Mrs. Thatcher noticed that her mind was preoccupied. She thought about Charles all the time, even daydreamed about the two of them getting married and living in a grand house. She couldn't concentrate and didn't have much of an appetite either.

***

When Sunday afternoon finally arrived, Mary waited impatiently by the creek until Charles came.

"Hello, Mary." He took her hand in his and kissed it,

giving her the attention she so desired. "You are the most beautiful woman in the South." He walked at her side and continued holding her hand in his.

"May I call you Charles? Mister is so formal."

"You may call me anything you'd like in private. People talk, you know."

"Yes. I do know, Charles. What do you want to talk to me about?"

"You're too beautiful to be living like a slave. You deserve better."

Mary's heart started pounding out of control, and she hoped he didn't hear it. "I feel that way too."

He placed a hand under her chin, lifted it, and kissed her lips. "You're dressed rather elegantly today—not like a slave."

"I have a few pretty things."

"You're lucky. Most girls like you don't have nice dresses. Did you get it from your master's daughter?"

"No. Becky doesn't speak to me at all."

"Why shouldn't she? You two being half-sisters and all."

"That's exactly why she hates me."

"How did you learn such perfect English?"

"I taught myself." Mary wasn't stupid enough to get Mrs. Thatcher involved.

"You're a smart girl. I've been living in the South all my life, and I haven't been able to shake the drawl."

He kissed her lips again. This time, his hand went to her breast.

"Stop. Don't touch me that way." She scurried away. "Is that all you want from me?"

"No. I'd like to get to know you."

She raucously said, "By touching me inappropriately?"

"I thought that's what you wanted?"

"Did I say that?"

"Sorry," he apologized.

"Why do we have to meet out here, rather than at your house?"

"I'll invite you over as a guest sometime."

"When?" she asked.

"Soon," he promised. "Here we can be alone. No formalities, just you and me."

Mary wanted Charles to like her, and she didn't want to run him away.

She allowed him to put an arm around her shoulder and kiss her neck. Her body was shaking, and she knew he felt it too. "You're seventeen. You should be thinking about getting married soon."

"I'd like to live in a grand house, host parties, go out on the town, and have lots of friends."

"You'll be the next Cinderella," he said, holding her hand in his. "Your life will improve, I promise. You'll have everything you want in life—a husband who loves you and children."

She frowned when he mentioned kids, knowing that some or all would probably be black or mulatto.

"How do you keep your hands so soft?"

She tried to relax but didn't succeed. "It's a secret."

"I bet the rest of you is soft too. Know what I like about you?" Charles asked. "You don't put on airs. I feel comfortable talking with you. I don't have to compete with other men who own large plantations. Women talk about luxury, and they don't care where it comes from. Not even if a man robs, kills, or gets his money from the backs of slaves."

"I want things too, Charles, but I'm not that picky." She flinched when he lightly bit her neck. "Yes, I've been thinking about getting married to a fine man who can give me everything in life I've ever wanted—things I deserve."

He smiled. "You deserve the best, Mary."

"And I shall have them." She knew he could give her everything her heart desired.

"I don't know you, Mary, but I love you."

Heat flashed within her. Those were the words she wanted to hear. She wanted him probably as badly as he wanted her.

She thought he would ask her to marry him, but the words never came.

Her mother had talked to her about men, and she hadn't listened. *After the problems I've had with men in the past, can I trust one again?*

Mary needed to think, had to get away from Charles for a while. "I have to go. See you next Sunday." She dashed away.

Chapter 9

Master Jimmy

SLAVES WORKED THE fields every day except Sunday. Master Boyd said they needed a day of rest, and Mrs. Thatcher gave Mary Sundays off as well. With nothing better to do, she rushed to the creek that morning to stash the five dollars she'd gotten from Mrs. Thatcher in her secret hiding place. Jimmy was swimming alone in the deep end of the creek. Mary had taught herself how to swim in the shallow part just by watching him. Charles wasn't due there until later that afternoon.

The bare-chested eight-year-old came out of the water when he saw her. He stood there in his underpants with water running off his body.

"Where are you going?" he asked.

"Can't I take a walk?"

"My daddy said you're not supposed to go anywhere alone. I'm telling. You'll get a whipping for sure."

"Today is your birthday, Jimmy. It's a time to be happy and kind to others, don't you think?"

"You'll address me as Mister or Master, slave. My daddy gave me a twenty-dollar gold piece for my birthday, and I can buy anything I'd like." The little boy picked up his trousers, pulled the new shiny coin from the pocket, and held it in his palm for her to see. "Bet you've never seen one, being a slave and all. My sister, Becky, said you think you're something, but you're nothing but a stinking black slave." He flipped the coin in front of her face, then shoved it back into the pocket of his pants. "My coin is just there, and you'd better not touch it either. I dare you." He walked out on a large log where white water was rushing over it. Water flew high into the air when he dove in, making a great splash.

Mary glanced around the area and saw no one else in sight. She hated the boy and had the chance to get rid of him forever. She'd already risked her life once. Now she was about to do it a second time. Picking up the boy's pants, she took the coin and dropped it into her pocket.

Jimmy swam back up to the log and yelled, "Hey. You better put that back."

Mary tucked her dress between her legs, walked out on the log, and dropped to her knees in front of Jimmy. "Make me, you little brat." She grabbed Jimmy by his hair, shoved his head under the water, and held him there until he stopped scratching and struggling. When she released him, he floated face down in the creek.

Walking a short distance away, she removed the top of the rotten stump, placed the five-dollar bill and the twenty-dollar gold piece into a small metal box, and closed it. She now had over five hundred dollars. Mary was not as stressed as when she'd killed Joe Joe. She smiled and hummed a cheerful melody all the way home.

***

When the doctor showed up at the big house, guests had started to arrive. Mary's mother said that Master Jimmy had drowned, and his entire family was grief-stricken. His mother had fainted, and the doctor gave her a sedative and demanded bedrest.

Jimmy's death was ruled an accidental drowning. They buried his body the next day. Everyone from the big house was dressed in black that morning. Mary watched the coffin leave the house, pulled by two white horses. The slaves gave their sympathy and mourned as well, crying over the little master's death.

Why would slaves have sympathy for those who held them in bondage and treated them like animals?

It actually was a joyful day for Mary. What did she care about Jimmy? He'd only grow up to be a slave master like his father.

Mary didn't meet Charles at the creek that Sunday. With a death in the big house, he'd understand.

***

Cyris sat on the porch with Mary, and she told him about freedom in the East and in Canada. He was interested in many things. She made him optimistic about a better future, and after talking, they had formed a bond. Cyris admitted he couldn't believe how sheltered and ignorant he was about what was going on in the world around him.

"How do you know all these things, Mary?" Cyris asked.

"I just do," she said.

"No other slaves know about such things."

"Masters like to keep us in the dark about what's going on in this country and the world. It's true, what I've told you," Mary said.

"Where are you getting this information?"

"I can't tell you. The South is no place for black people. Back East, they don't have slaves. You can live free—get a job where they pay you to work like white people—and no longer be a slave and work long hours for nothing. You can go to school, learn how to read, and find your own place to live. Black families live together. Do you know your mother, Cyris?"

"No," he admitted. "Don't recall her at all. They took me away from her before I was six. Kind of been on my own since then."

"Except for your fellow slaves, you're all alone in this world."

"Where is the best place to go, Mary?"

"Canada. Never tell anyone what we've talked about, especially the other slaves. You can't trust them. Why, they don't even dream about freedom. But there are black folks out there who will help you escape. Don't trust anyone in the South. They'll turn you in within a blink of an eye."

Mary spoke about freedom, but she was vague, not wanting to get into trouble herself if Master Boyd found out.

Cyris was almost a year older than Mary was, and yet she knew so much more than he did. Maybe people told her things because she looked white and pretty. She told him colorful stories about faraway places as if she'd actually been to them. He believed she truly would end up in New York City. He expected to find her missing someday, gone without a trace, and he'd know she was free.

CHAPTER 10

MARY'S SECRET BEAU

THE FOLLOWING SUNDAY, Mary met Charles at the usual place, same time.

She rushed to hug him. "Sorry about last week. With a death in the family, I'm sure you understand."

"Awful thing," Charles said. "Sad indeed. Jimmy was so young."

He kissed her. "I love you, Mary. You're the woman I want to marry."

He tried her breast again, and this time she didn't resist. His soft touch stimulated her. He opened her dress, and his tongue caressed her nipples. Excitement rushed through her like the water in the nearby creek. Then his hand went between her legs. Again, she didn't resist. Next thing she knew they were on the ground, and he was on top of her. After their lovemaking, he said he had to go. It was as if he'd lost all interest in her.

"Don't leave, Charles. I want to talk to you about us."

He raised his eyebrows. "Us?"

"Where will we live, Charles? I need to get my freedom from Master Boyd."

"Tell you what. Think about it, and we'll discuss it later."

He rushed off, promising to see her next Sunday—same time, same place.

"Do you love me, Charles?" she called after him.

"Yes, Mary. I love you very much," he replied.

Mary was ecstatic. She had a young man in her life who loved her. They would get married, and he would take her from the humiliating and demeaning world she despised. She would live like a white woman, wear grand dresses, and host parties. She couldn't wait to see Charles again. She hugged herself, threw her head back, and giggled. She'd show her mother and Walter. Maybe she didn't need to travel to New York City after all. Everything she wanted was at her feet, right here in New Orleans.

***

When Mary showed up at Mrs. Thatcher's house that Monday morning, the woman was working in a rather large, freshly dug garden. She said it was her pride and joy, but the slaves did most of the work. She wore a huge, floppy straw hat, gloves, and a pair of boots. She tilled soil around three tomato plants. She had a bucket of water and chicken manure for fertilizer. She'd dug a trench in the middle of one of the rows and dropped in okra seeds.

"My driver got most of my seeds and plants from your plantation," she said to Mary. "When you plant tomatoes, plant them deep. It won't hurt them. The same way with squash and other plants. They absorb water better that way."

"I see lots of okra seeds," Mary said.

"I just planted a whole row. There's a restaurant in town that makes the best fried okra I've ever had."

The old woman was huffing and puffing, and Mary just hoped she wouldn't faint.

Mary stood at the edge of the garden, avoiding the loose soil. "Want me to help you with that?"

"No. I can manage, dear."

"It looks like hard work. Why don't you have the men do this?"

"It's my garden. I couldn't ask them to take care of it."

Mary wondered why Mrs. Thatcher never visited her plantation. Other masters and their wives, from as far away as Texas and Mississippi, showed up sometimes.

"I have some things for you to do in the house, Mary. Clean up the kitchen and mop the floor, honey. Then come outside, sit under the shade tree, and read to me."

"Yes, ma'am, Mrs. Thatcher."

***

Mrs. Thatcher's daughter and her children had returned almost as fast as they'd disappeared, arriving on the noon stage—just the three of them this time. Even Mrs. Thatcher didn't know they were coming. No one mentioned Mr. Edward, and Mary certainly didn't plan to bring up the subject.

Mary served tea and cookies, while Mrs. Thatcher cried over her daughter and the little ones' return.

Mary enjoyed playing with the kids. They consumed most of her time. She changed the baby, fed both kids, and had nonstop playtime with the three-year-old.

Diane said, "Mary, we're going out to lunch."

Mary had a difficult time keeping up with supper and dinner. Both meant different meals to people in the South, but lunch was not a problem. "Don't worry about the kids. I'll take real good care of them."

"We want you to come with us," Diane said.

A nerve rattled within Mary. "I can't go."

"Why not? No one knows you're black," Mrs. Thatcher added.

Mary cringed. "Master Boyd might be there."

"I'm sure he won't say a word," Diane said.

"But the kids?"

Diane snickered. "Kids eat in restaurants all the time."

"You have new dresses here," Mrs. Thatcher said. "Wear one."

Mary burst into nervous laughter. "Are you sure?"

"Positive," Diane said.

Mary couldn't hold her excitement as she rushed upstairs and changed. Goosebumps covered her body as she rode into town. This day she'd enter a restaurant as a white woman—for the second time. The waiters would treat her with the utmost respect, as a Southern Belle with money.

John parked the carriage outside, and all three women entered the restaurant. Mary's eyes scanned the place, looking for someone who might recognize her. She saw no one. Using a handheld fan, she fanned herself constantly but still dripped sweat. A waiter led them to a table in the center of the place.

"This is so much fun," Mary said. Diane's presence made it more intriguing. "I feel lightheaded."

"Try to relax," Diane said.

Mrs. Thatcher tried to calm Mary. "It's nothing special, just eating lunch somewhere other than at home. You've done it before."

Everyone in the place stared at Mary, which made her even more nervous.

"Why are they staring?" Mary asked.

"Because you're the most beautiful female in the place, and they don't recognize you. Look around … the other women don't fair nearly as well as you," Mrs. Thatcher said.

"Am I really that beautiful?" Mary asked.

"Don't you look in the mirror every now and then?" Diane asked.

Mary glanced around the room again, and almost every man there had his eye on her, young and old.

"You need to leave the South," Diane said. "You could be a famous play actor in New York City and travel the world. Things could work out for you."

Such potentials made Mary's heart flutter. "You think so?"

"Yes," Mrs. Thatcher agreed.

Diane said, "Go for the good life, Mary. You'd be a fool if you don't take it."

Just then, a young man eagerly made his way to their table. "Hello, Mrs. Thatcher. Who are these lovely ladies in your company?"

Mrs. Thatcher smiled and said, "This is my daughter, Diane, from New York City, and my niece, Mary. They're visiting me for a few weeks. And these two little fellows are Diane's kids."

"Nice kids," he said.

"You ladies are very lovely," he added, keeping his eyes on Mary. "May I visit your plantation sometime, Mrs. Thatcher, and take these ladies on a tour of the countryside?"

"I'm afraid that's not possible," Mrs. Thatcher said. "My daughter's children keep her busy and Mary helps me around the house."

"Don't you have slaves to do that, Mrs. Thatcher?"

Mary interjected. "Thanks for inviting us. What my aunt is trying to say is that I'm engaged to be married and wandering around the country with another man is not respectable."

"Point taken. Ladies." He bowed and left.

Mary didn't like him anyway. He was too flashy, too sure of himself—a ladies' man.

When he left, other men gathered around him, inquisitive about his conversation. The not-available flag went up, and other men stayed clear, but that didn't stop them from staring.

Mary realized that she didn't have a purse, just like the time Master Boyd had left her in town. All women carried purses. On her next outing, she'd have a purse with five dollars in it.

"There are not many people in here," Mary noted, "and the restaurant down the street is closed."

"I've heard there's an epidemic going around. Lots of people are sick," Mrs. Thatcher commented.

"Is it contagious?" Diane asked.

"The doctors said not to worry."

"What is it?" Mary asked.

"Don't know. I heard the hospital is crowded," Mrs. Thatcher said. "The authorities don't want to start a panic."

"Maybe we shouldn't eat here," Diane said. "I don't want the children to get sick."

"Do you want to leave?" Mrs. Thatcher asked.

"Yes," her daughter replied.

"How about you, Mary?"

"I don't want to get sick either. Maybe we should go."

They left the restaurant, went back home, and prepared lunch.

***

Mary lay on the grass with Charles at the creek after he'd had his way with her twice.

She sat up next to him and smiled. "When can we get married, Charles?"

"Married?" He threw his head back and laughed. "You're a slave. No white man in his right mind will marry you."

Her smile evaporated, and her pulse began to race. "Slave …?"

"I planned to keep our relationship going until I could buy you from Mr. Boyd. But your price is mighty high."

Mary dolefully shook her head. "Buy me? Like an animal?"

"You're a slave. Yes, you're sort of an animal. Property. You'd live in the house with us. Under the same roof."

Anger flared throughout her body. "Live with your mother and sister? Be your slave?"

"Not my sister, my fiancée. You saw her the first time we met."

"I thought she was your sister," Mary hissed.

"We'll be married next month. She's a thoroughbred and doesn't have a slave for a mother."

Mary bellowed, "She's not even pretty."

"She's white, pure white, and her family owns a plantation much larger than ours. She can give me fine children."

Mary's stomach lurched, and she began to shake. The tears came, and she couldn't stop them. "Why did you pretend to love me? You lied to me. I would've never let you touch me if I had known."

"I love you as a slave, a companion. Not as a wife."

She screamed at him, and her eyes narrowed. "You said we could get married." She tried to stand, but her legs became too weak to support her weight.

"I meant in a pretend way," he said with a haughty glare. "We can take our vows. 'Til death do us part."

"No," she said defiantly. Her jaw tightened in anger. "I won't be your wench."

His voice was taut as he said, "You can only give birth to black heathens I can sell off as property. Do you think you can fit into a white world because of your looks? Why, even the white men back East won't take you for a wife. It's ludicrous. I have to go, Mary." He kissed her lips and stood. "See you next Sunday."

She summoned a smile. "I'll be here."

He climbed to his feet and swaggered away.

Mary stood on shaky legs and brushed off her dress. Shocked by his statement, she cried all the way home. She had been stupid enough to think he loved her. She was nothing more to him than a slave.

***

The next Sunday afternoon, Mary met Charles at the creek, carrying a knife in the pocket of her old black dress. The knife wasn't as large as Mike's, but it was sharper. She'd get even with that bastard. He'd used her and wanted her for his wench, but he'd never touch her or another woman again.

"Hello, beautiful." He smiled and presented her with good news. "Your master has agreed to sell you to me. Isn't that wonderful? Now we can be together forever."

She couldn't even force a smile, and her nostrils flared. "What would your wife think?"

"Wives prefer their husbands to have affairs with slaves, because they'd never leave them for one. It's like having a woman on the side who doesn't threaten their marriage. Don't you agree, Mary?"

All the hate and disappointment hit her like a hurricane. "Yes," Mary said. Pulling the knife out of her pocket, she swiftly slit Charles's throat twice.

With his mouth wide open, shock and fear clouded his face. The death rattle of blood gurgled from the gaping wound and flowed down the front of his shirt. His knees buckled, and he fell to the ground, clutching his throat. His eyes darkened into an intense stare. A red puddle formed under him and grew larger as Mary stood there watching for a while. She washed her face and hands in the creek, tossed the knife into the bubbling white water where she'd drowned Jimmy, and walked home.

She'd never trust another man again.

**

A slave discovered Master Charles's body two days later. The authorities scoured the area, looking for evidence involving another mysterious murder at the creek. There was an inquest, and the authorities questioned almost everyone except Mary. Why was he there, so far from home? Throat slashed twice was what Mary had heard, and he'd bled out quickly. Very few people visited the creek anyway. Now no one went there. Jimmy had drowned there under mysterious circumstances. Joe Joe's body was discovered there and now Charles's. After the slaying of Mr. Charles, the authorities weren't so sure of Mike's guilt. Mary discovered that Mike had hanged for Joe Joe's murder.

CHAPTER 11

CYRIS'S FRIENDS

CYRIS HAD THREE good friends about his age. He conjured up enough courage to discuss running away with them. He told them about freedom in the East and in Canada. They listened with enthusiasm, but they weren't willing to run away.

"We're not watched at this plantation like slaves at other places. We can do it if we stick together," Cyris pleaded. "Master Boyd has us deliver vegetables and horses to other places. We could take off then."

"No," one said, and the rest shook their heads. "Runaway slaves get hanged or whipped to death."

"Will you just think about it? We can discuss it later. I'll give you until next Sunday," Cyris said.

"Where are four black boys going to hide?" one asked.

"I understand there are people out there who will help us. Hide us. Get us to New York or Canada."

"No," one said, then the others.

Cyris tried convincing the other boys. "There's a whole new world out there. We have to try. At least think about a better future."

"We don't know how to read or write. We have no money and wouldn't know how to count it if we did. Four black boys traveling together will look suspicious. It can't be done," the same boy said adamantly.

"If we had transportation and someone to look after us …" another one said.

"Who's going to look after us but ourselves?" Cyris asked.

After lunch, the head overseer and three black overseers fetched Cyris from his room. "Come with us, boy."

They led him into the yard, out of earshot from the other slaves. "We've heard talk about you wanting to run away. Is this true?"

Cyris gasped for air. "What do you mean?"

"You're trying to convince others to run away with you. That makes you a troublemaker. We don't like troublemakers, boy. Where did you get this idea? Who's been putting things into your head?"

Horror and anger etched in Cyris's mind. "Nobody, suh. Honest."

"When we get through with you, you'll tell. Tie him to the tree, boys."

One of the black overseers ripped Cyris's shirt from his back, while the other two tied his hands around a large tree. Cyris had witnessed black men whipped there by overseers in the past, but he never thought it would happen to him.

"You're going to get a whipping, boy," the man holding the whip said. "It can be a light whipping or a death whipping. Which do you prefer?"

Slaves filed out of their quarters and watched—men, women, and children. He was an example for all who thought or talked about freedom. His friends and fellow slaves had betrayed him. Mary warned him not to trust them, to keep his mouth shut. He couldn't snitch on her. Today, they would whip him to death. If he told on Mary, they'd whip her too. Then she would have to give up her source. He knew it was Mrs. Thatcher. There could be no one else.

The first blow from the whip took off his skin. The pain was unbearable. Other lashes followed in rapid succession. Cyris screamed. The pain was so severe he wet his pants. More lashes followed. He thought the whipping would never stop, but it did. "Where are you getting this information from, boy?"

He had an urge to tell … anything to stop the pain. "Nobody, I tell you. Nobody."

The lashes started again. Sometime during his beatings, Cyris lost consciousness. He woke up lying face down in the dirt in more pain than he'd ever thought possible. But he was still alive.

Two men dragged Cyris into the room he shared with

eight others. He lay on his stomach, knowing the stinging pain from the lashes on his back would end like all bad things in his life—except being a slave. He whimpered and cried like a child, hating the other slaves for turning him in, simply because he spoke about fleeing. He got double lashes because he refused to tell where he got his idea about freedom. What was worse, the overseer who'd whipped him was black like him. The man's face revealed no emotion, as if it was carved in stone.

A small boy entered the room with a pan of water and gently blotted the blood from Cyris's back with a wet cloth. The men stayed outside, and everything was eerily quiet. How could they be so stupid as to let themselves be slaves without trying to escape—without trying to seek a better life? It was just as Mary had said. Most slaves had no idea how things were in different parts of the country because their masters kept them in the dark. That was no excuse for their ignorance. Except for Mary, he felt all alone in the world.

No relatives, no friends, no one he could trust.

***

A week after Cyris's whipping, he found Mary walking along the creek.

"Hello, Mary," he said. "Is it safe for you to be out here all alone?"

"About as safe as anywhere, I guess. I heard about your whipping."

"I didn't tell them nothing about you—where I got my idea about running away and all."

"I know. Folks have seen us talking. They think I'm the source, but they have no proof."

Cyris glanced into the water. "Do you know how to swim, Mary?"

"Taught myself."

He grinned from ear to ear. "I knew it. I knew you could swim. Can you teach me sometime?"

"Sure, but how can you explain returning to your quarters all wet?"

"I'll tell them I played in the shallow end of the creek."

"They'll believe that."

"How about teaching me now?" he asked.

"I can't do it now. We both can't walk back wet."

"We don't have to walk back together. You go first, then I'll follow."

She shook her head. "No, you know how people talk."

He anxiously removed his shirt and shoes. "Can you tell me?"

"Have you watched Jimmy swim?"

"Yes," Cyris said.

"That's the way I learned. Get into the shallow end. Hold your breath and do what you saw Jimmy do. You remember how he used his arms and legs?"

"Yes."

"Get in, hold your breath, and float first, just to get used to the water."

Cyris waded out to where the water came up to his waist, lay down on the surface and floated, holding his breath. He stood up. "I can float."

"Sure you can. All you need to do now is move your arms and legs like Jimmy did. Hold your breath and do it."

Cyris did. Arms up and over as if he were reaching, then down, and he repeated the motion. He moved his legs up and down for as long as he could hold his breath. When he stood, he was at the bank.

He'd just made the biggest accomplishment of his life. "Did you see me, Mary? I did it. I moved all this way."

"Do it a few more times," she said. "Get familiar with the water. You'll feel more comfortable."

Cyris walked over to where the water came to his shoulders. Leaning over, he held his breath and swam back to shore. He stood and laughed. "I can do it."

"The hardest part is learning how to breathe," Mary said. "Try it again. This time, when your opposite arm is in the air, turn your head to one side and take a breath."

Cyris tried it and swallowed water. He stood up, coughing.

"Keep your eyes open so you can see where the water level is. You only need to do it a few times before you get it right."

Cyris was reluctant to try again. "I think I've had enough for today."

"Come on, Cyris. Try it again. You're doing so well."

He stood, breathed heavily for a moment, and tried to catch his breath.

"Cyris."

He coughed out, "Just a minute."

He took about a five-minute break before he tried to swim again. He waded to the same spot and started swimming. This time he took a breath with his head held high out of the water. He did it repeatedly until he reached the bank.

"Yahoo," he shouted. "I can swim."

Mary clapped her hands and laughed. "Try it again."

Cyris swam all around the creek, both the shallow and deep ends. He played in the water for half an hour before he gave up. Learning how to swim gave him a new outlook on life. Running away could be just as easy. All he had to do was try.

"Don't let anyone know you can swim. If they find out, tell them you taught yourself," Mary said.

He laughed aloud and threw his hands into the air. "I won't tell a soul, Mary."

Mary allowed him to walk back to his quarters a few minutes ahead of her.

CHAPTER 12

YELLOW JACK

MOST PEOPLE IN the countryside didn't know about the invisible stalker that went from house to house until it had touched the lives of everyone, rich and poor. Citizens of every rank fled the city in haste, riding in carts, carriages, and wagons. They flocked to the countryside in every direction. The poor, and those who had no relatives in the countryside, remained within town, too afraid to leave their homes.

But things got worse. No matter where citizens went, the fever followed. The epidemic was growing worse— and winning.

Mary hadn't known about yellow jack until all the roads from New Orleans were shut down. Men with rifles blocked all passageways to and from the area, threatening to shoot anyone who attempted to leave. Everyone was petrified, including the masters and all occupants of their mansions. The city was under quarantine: the first time Mary had ever heard the word. She didn't understand the problem until Mrs. Thatcher told her the truth.

"Doctors call it yellow fever. Most of the victims are white people, very few slaves. They call it yellow jack, because the patient's skin usually turns yellow. They have a loss of appetite and can't keep anything down. They are in constant pain and bleed from their noses, mouths, and eyes. Their vomit is black," Mrs. Thatcher said. She sat under a large oak tree in the backyard as she usually did, sipping her evening tea. "Why, it's horrible. No one knows what causes it, and there's no cure. People in town are dying on the streets, and the authorities kept it a secret until thousands died."

Mary cringed. "Can it spread here?"

"It's everywhere. There was a doctor at the Crawford's place two weeks ago. I had John drive me over there. Jill, Mr. Crawford's sister, is the closest friend I have here. I knew someone was home, but they wouldn't open the door. I haven't seen or heard from her in over a month."

"Why did the authorities keep it a secret?" Mary asked. "People have a right to know."

"They didn't want to cause a panic." The woman grunted. "Isn't that silly? That's why some restaurants were closed the last time we went into town."

"If everyone had known earlier—"

"I saw wagons, carriages, and omnibuses stretched for almost a mile after thousands had succumbed to the disease. The streets were empty when we drove through. Businesses had closed their doors to the public, and people were dying on the streets like mangy dogs. I don't think I'll ever go into town again."

***

All fieldwork had stopped, except for hoeing cotton. Today was Cyris's turn to work in the fields. The hot sun beamed down on him while he hoed grass and weeds from around the stalks as fast as he could. Overseers on horseback watched the slaves work. If overseers thought slaves were working too slowly, they'd get a lash from a whip to speed them up.

The fastest woman was allergic to bees, but she could hoe as well as any man. Each time she got stung, she was off work sick for about a week. A bee stung her, not once, but several times.

The woman screamed and summoned the guard, who galloped his horse down the row toward her.

"What's wrong with you, gal? Don't give me that bee sting story just because you don't want to work."

"She's allergic," Cyris said.

"Mind your own business, boy. Who told you to stop working?"

Cyris started hoeing again. "The doctor said—" The whip across his back, mixed with sweat, burned into his wound.

"I don't want no lip from you again, boy. And you, woman. I'm tired of you trying to get out of work."

As the woman started hoeing again, Cyris saw welts on her face and arms, but she continued working. Half an hour later, she collapsed.

The man rode back on his horse. "Stop that. Get up and get back to work." His whip struck the woman four times, but she didn't move. The man dismounted and turned her over. "Get up."

Still, the woman didn't move. Cyris helped the overseer pick her up and lay her across his horse. He left the field with her lying motionless over his saddle.

That night, they buried her. They said Master Boyd was upset about losing one of his best workers.

***

Cyris had a few days' rest. They didn't pick any vegetables, but he didn't know the reason why until he went to search for Mary. She was sitting on a block of wood under the big tree in her front yard, as she did most of the time when she was home.

"Hello, Mary," Cyris said. "How've you been?"

"The same," she said. "Nothing changes around here."

He sat on a block of wood near her. "We're not working so hard anymore, except for hoeing cotton. Vegetables are rotting in the fields."

"If I tell you, Cyris, promise me you won't tell a soul."

"I didn't listen to you once, Mary. I won't be that stupid again."

"There's a disease, yellow fever, but everybody calls it yellow jack. It has spread all over New Orleans. No one can travel in or out of this area. My family doesn't even know about it."

"Disease? How do I know if I get it?"

"It only attacks white folks, Cyris. You won't contract the disease."

"What about you, Mary? Being half-white, I mean."

"I don't know," she said.

Cyris got a warm feeling in the pit of his stomach. Maybe there was a god after all, and he was punishing white folks for the way they treated Cyris and his people. Maybe they'd all die, and he would be free from hard work.

"What causes this disease?" he asked.

Mary shrugged nonchalantly. "No one knows, but until it stops, nothing leaves or enters New Orleans—not people, not anything. Ships don't dock there anymore. It hit the city the hardest. Shops are closed, and the streets are empty."

***

It was mid-July, and white folks were dropping like flies from the fever.

Mary had planned to tell Mrs. Thatcher about the life

she had growing inside of her, but when she arrived at the house, the woman was sick in bed.

"Mrs. Thatcher," Mary asked, "what's wrong?"

"I don't feel well," Mrs. Thatcher said between agonizing gasps. "Dear, send John for the doctor. My stomach feels as if it's burning up."

Mary panicked. *What if Mrs. Thatcher has yellow jack?*

The doctors sent word that they had too many patients. One would be there as soon as he could. Mary spent that night with Mrs. Thatcher, and the woman got sicker.

Mary tried to feed her, but she only threw it up.

"I have the fever, honey. I know the symptoms."

"You can't be sure until the doctor says so," Mary said.

"I feel so bad. I'm dying."

Mary held her hand. She had never thought of Mrs. Thatcher dying. "No, Mrs. Thatcher, you're going to be all right."

Tears flowed from Mary's eyes, and she couldn't stop them. The woman was almost like a mother to her, and Mary couldn't stand the thought of her dying.

Finally, a doctor showed up about noon the next day. Mary stayed outside the room until he completed his examination. When the doctor walked out, he looked at Mary and shook his head. "You her kin?"

"No," Mary said. "Her children live back East. I just help out around here."

"She has the fever, my child."

Mary gasped, "She's dying?"

"Unless we find a cure and in a hurry, I'm afraid so."

"Does she know?"

"Yes. Her folks can't come here. Said you are her closest kin."

"But I can't remain here. I might catch it too."

"Some people contract the disease; some don't," he said. "All you can do is make her comfortable. I left two bottles of laudanum on the nightstand. Give her a teaspoonful every four hours."

Mary loved Mrs. Thatcher, but not enough to die for her. "If she's infected, I can't stay here."

"This house is under quarantine. You can't leave here and spread it to others, like your family. Where do you live?" the doctor asked.

Mary pointed. "The next plantation, over there."

"Use a cold, damp cloth to keep her face and arms cool. I'll stop in next door and let them know you won't be returning."

Josh didn't pick her up that evening. She waited, but he didn't show until the next day. He brought her clothes and a message from Master Boyd: "Stay with Mrs. Thatcher until she passes."

Mrs. Thatcher got sicker and sicker.

Mary became emotionally weaker and weaker.

The doctor dropped in and left more medicine for Mrs. Thatcher. He asked Mary how she felt. How did he expect her to feel? She was frightened to death. Mary had watched her patient's skin turn yellow. The woman couldn't eat, and if she did, she threw it up. She bled from her eyes and mouth. Sometimes she was coherent, other times she talked out of her head.

Mrs. Thatcher removed her wedding ring and a diamond necklace she wore at all times and placed them into Mary's hands. "Take these. Go east to New York or north to Canada. You know where I keep my cash. I have lots of it. Take it all and start a new life, my child. I should have listened to you and moved back East. Now I'll never see my children again, and they can't visit me here. I'm dying, Mary, and I'm in so much pain."

Mary cried out, "What can I do for you, Mrs. Thatcher?"

"Write letters to my children," she said.

Mary glanced around the large room. "I'll write it all down. Everything you want me to."

"If I tell you, can you remember it?"

Mary nodded.

"I need to get something off my chest, Mary. When my husband and I first got married, he traveled a lot. I got lonely, had an affair with another man. My son, my oldest child, is not my husband's boy. He's Master Boyd's son."

"Mrs. Thatcher, there's no need for your son to know that. What's it going to help?" Mary thought about the life she had growing inside her.

"I want my son to know who his father is."

"Does Master Boyd know?" Mary asked.

"Yes. He was like a father to my son until his first wife found out. Don't know how, but she figured it out. Probably because they look so much alike. That's why we haven't been welcome there in years."

"If you want me to tell him, I will, but I don't see a need to, Mrs. Thatcher."

Would her son be like Master Boyd, an arrogant low-life who believed that people with darker skin were animals, less than the whites?

"I tried to purchase you, Mary, but your father refused to sell you. Said he could get more for you than any other female slave. Said he had something planned for you. He wouldn't say what. He was furious when I told him I planned to set you free to live in the East. You're his daughter, honey. But he thinks of you only as a slave."

Mary already knew what the woman said was true. "Thanks for trying to help me, Mrs. Thatcher. You're the nicest person I've ever met. Your daughter is nice too. I really like Diane."

"She divorced that no-good husband of hers. I'm so sorry for what he did to you, Mary. We never blamed you. The only reason he didn't succeed in raping you is because we decided not to eat lunch in town. You have my daughter's address. Contact her when you get to New York City. Promise me you'll leave right after my death."

"But you're not going to die," Mary cried, not sure if she was trying to convince the woman or herself.

Mary sat at Mrs. Thatcher's side, rocking back and forth and crying hysterically. The woman looked like talking death, and Mary was afraid for both of them.

"I'm in so much pain, Mary," she said. "I have a bad headache, and my body aches all over. How can I be so hot and shivering at the same time? I know I'm dying, Mary, and it's an awful way to go."

The terrified Mary accompanied Mrs. Thatcher to the death camp at Alligator Island, riding on a wagon filled with fever victims all around her. With all the sickness and death, Mary knew she had no chance of survival. Black puke and blood spattered all over her from many of the victims. The drivers and caretakers were all slaves, like herself. Many asked, "Why is a white woman in such a forsaken place?"

Mrs. Thatcher shared one of many white tents filled with other patients. Mary sat at her side, holding her hand and talking to her, but the woman was delirious most of the time. Then she rolled her eyes, her chest stopped moving, and her hand went limp. She was gone.

Mary didn't think she had any more tears left, but she cried. Of all the awful, mean white people in the world, why did a wonderful person like Mrs. Thatcher have to die? She was Mary's friend—her mentor.

Mary followed a loaded wagon to the gravesite, where they threw Mrs. Thatcher into a trench with other victims who had died from the fever. There was no grave marker or funeral. They covered the dead like discarded animals.

A fine lady like Mrs. Thatcher deserved better.

Mary wanted to go into the water and wash, but alligators were everywhere; most were small, but larger ones lurked somewhere beneath the dark abyss.

She spent almost two weeks on the island of death, comforting the dying. Many patients gave her their jewelry and asked her to write letters to their family members who couldn't visit. Letters couldn't leave New Orleans, because doctors didn't know how the disease spread. Since all communication from New Orleans to the rest of the country had ceased, Mary put the jewelry and letters into envelopes with the owner's name on them. When the fever ended, she'd make sure their relatives received those last precious connections with their loved ones.

***

But Mary had another mission. She wanted to kill Master Boyd, and she had thought about it repeatedly. She knew she could poison him if she could get into the big house. First, he had treated her like a wench. Then, he had sent her off to die such a horrible death. Now, thoughts about how to plan his death consumed her mind. She hated him and wanted him to suffer like the dying around her.

The slaves took shifts. Mary worked twelve hours per day, seven days a week. After supper, she usually fell on a cot and passed out. The mumbling, sobbing, and other noises no longer kept her up at night. She was tired of patients throwing up and bleeding all over her. She never touched her food with her hands, only using utensils. She washed her hands constantly. She felt sick herself, but not from the fever. Incurable fatigue and depression plagued her body.

Chapter 13

The Abortionist

MARY WAS TWO months with child when she made her way back to Mrs. Thatcher's house and collected the cash the woman had promised. Mary took only half the money and left more than enough cash for Mrs. Thatcher's slaves to survive on until her children could take over the plantation.

The three-mile walk through the woods ended at the box she'd stashed in the stump. Since the box now held so much paper money, she could hardly close its lid. She smiled.

She took the same path back. When she returned to Mrs. Thatcher's house, she found John relaxing on the front steps of the house he shared with the two other servants.

"Hello, John," she said, sitting on the step next to him.

"Mary. How're you today?"

"I need your help."

"You need to go someplace?" he asked.

"Yes, but I need you to tell me where."

"I don't get it," he said.

"John, I'm in trouble."

"What kind of trouble?"

"I'm with child, John, and I don't want the baby. I've heard there are women who know how to end a pregnancy. Since you drive a lot, I thought maybe you'd know of one."

"I've heard of several women in this area who are good for such ailments. The best one is a woman who lives in the swamps. I've never met her, but she used to be a slave."

"Do you know where she lives?"

"I've seen the house she lives in. It's out a ways."

"Can you take me there now?" Mary didn't want the thing growing in her body, and she wanted to get rid of it as soon as possible.

He stood. "Sure. She's going to expect you to pay her. Don't know how much."

"I can pay."

"Let's go," he said, walking toward the barn. "It'll take me a few minutes to hitch up my rig."

Mary followed John to the barn and watched him hitch up his team. She climbed on the seat with him, and they headed for the abortionist.

"This woman's a spiritual reader and healer," John

said. "She tells people's fortunes. All of her clients are white people. They claim she once helped a man walk again."

"She doesn't treat black people?"

"Slaves ain't got no money or transportation."

The well-traveled road had many wagon tracks. Small streams trickled across the road where water had pooled alongside it. The farther they drove, the narrower the road became and the larger the bodies of water became. Trees grew thick but not tall, and moss hung from some of the branches and trunks. Small gators and snakes were plentiful.

Their journey ended at an old shack in the middle of the swamps. Nothing else was in sight. Mary didn't see a horse or a wagon, and she wondered how the woman left the place. The house sat about six feet off the ground on stilts, and a small alligator ran under it.

An old black woman sitting on the porch was the spitting image of Mrs. Thatcher's housemaid, Hattie May. She sat in a rocking chair, holding something in her lap. The woman leaned back, then rocked a bit.

John stepped down from the wagon and walked up the steps. "Morning, ma'am," he said. "This is Mary. She has a problem she needs to get rid of. Can you help her?"

The woman nodded and turned her attention to Mary. "The name's Annie May, honey. How far along are you?"

"Two months," Mary said.

"Yes." The woman nodded again. "I can help you.

You'll have to stay here for at least three days. Can you do that?"

Mary stepped down from the wagon and ran up to the porch, fearing the alligator would chase her. "I didn't bring a change of clothes."

"You won't need them," Annie May said, then added, "Never run from a gator or any wild animal. You can't outrun them—and running means you're afraid. Just makes them chase you faster."

The woman wore a faded yellow dress, and gray braids hung down her back. She was too old to keep for a slave—and she had to be Hattie May's twin sister. She was sitting on her rickety porch, shelling green peas in a bowl. She smiled, but Mary saw apprehension in her weathered eyes.

"Pick her up in three days, around noon," Annie May said to John as she stood and opened the front door for Mary.

"You come back and get me, you hear," Mary yelled at John's back.

"I will," he said. After looking curiously under the house, he rushed to his wagon and drove off.

Words strained with desperation, Mary said. "I can't be left here. I don't know where I am."

"He'll be back, honey," the woman promised.

Annie May held open the door and allowed Mary to enter.

Alligator and rattlesnake heads covered the walls

in the living room. Three lit candles flickered in a red, green, and yellow glass bowl, giving the place a ghostly appearance. In the room was an old divan, a small table with four chairs, and a wood-burning heater with junk piled on it.

"I charge twenty dollars." Annie May wanted her money up front.

Mary gave her a twenty-dollar bill, and the lady led her into a back room in the shack.

"Come on in here and strip from the waist down. It ain't much of a house or a room, but it's clean. I can get rid of the baby, honey, but I can't guarantee you'll ever be able to have more. Some women do, some don't."

"Just get rid of it," Mary said.

A small table stood at the bedside with a black oil lamp in the center. The woman closed the curtains and lit the lamp, bringing a faint glow to the dark room. The faded covers were clean, and towels lined where the lower part of Mary's body would rest. There was a chifforobe with a missing wardrobe door on one wall and a bureau on the other side of the room. Mary undressed as instructed and lay on a lumpy mattress held up by wooden slats.

Annie May left the room for a few minutes and returned with something that looked like a ball of dried herbs. "Lie on your back and spread your legs, honey."

Mary obeyed. The woman shoved the contents as far up Mary's vagina as possible with a wooden spoon. "It'll take two days," the woman said. "You'll feel some cramping, but that's normal. It means the medicine is working. When the baby comes out, you'll bleed a lot. That's normal too."

"Will I get sick?" Mary asked.

"Sick to your stomach until the baby is gone. Then you'll feel better."

There was a knock at the door, and Annie May went to see who was calling.

"Hello," Mary heard her say. "Come on in and have a seat."

Then her voice went so low Mary couldn't hear the conversation.

For the time being, Mary lay still but didn't feel a thing.

Late that night the cramping began, and she felt like throwing up.

The woman came in to check up on her. "How do you feel?"

"Bad," Mary whined.

"That's part of the process. It's going to get worse."

"It hurts so badly."

"We can't reverse it. You just have to deal with the pain."

Mary had trouble sleeping that night. The woman gave her a bitter hot tea for the cramping, but it didn't work. The next morning, she doubled the dosage, and Mary felt some relief.

Mary had nothing to think about except planning her future. As soon as the quarantine lifted, she was going to be on the next stage or ship out of New Orleans. She had enough money and the right kind of clothes to pass as a white woman. She spoke proper English and had no reason to remain in the South. She would miss her siblings and her mother, but not Walter. Once she settled back East, she would purchase her entire family and move them in with her. *Mama won't have to work anymore. I'll even buy Walter, if that's what Mama wants me to do.* She would learn how to act, sing, and dance. With all her bad memories left behind in the South, she could start anew. She even planned to find Mr. Edward and make him pay for what he'd done to her.

While Mary lay in the back room, guests came and went.

Annie May was right about her medicine. After two days, the worst was over. Mary felt something slip down her vagina and the bleeding started.

"That's the baby," the woman said. She removed it from between Mary's legs.

Mary closed her eyes and turned her head. She didn't want to see the awful creature.

"That's it?" Mary asked. Almost instantly, the cramping stopped.

"Yes. It's all over, honey. Rest here for tonight. Try to eat some soup. Tomorrow you can go home. Remember to take it easy for a few days. Don't do anything to strain yourself, you hear?"

"Annie May, do you have a twin sister named Hattie May?"

"Yes. We were sold to different owners when we were about eight years old." The woman's voice became anxious. "Do you know her? Is she still alive?"

"I know a woman named Hattie May, and I can take you to her. She looks exactly like you, but she's not as agile."

"Agile?"

"She doesn't get around well."

"Who owns her?"

"No one at the moment."

The woman's eyes filled with joy. "When your driver gets back, I want to visit her, if I can."

"You can, and you shall, Annie May. I'm not white. My mother is black."

"I knew something was different the minute the driver called you by your first name." Annie May reached out and ran her fingers through Mary's hair. "You look whiter than white folks. Well, I'll be."

"When the new owners return, Hattie May will need a place to live. She's too old and fragile to work."

"Why, she can live here with me. I'd love to have her company."

"You don't know if she's really your sister."

"She'll know our mother's name. And I'll know if it's her."

They sat on the porch and talked from morning until noon. Mary confided in the woman—told her all about her life on the plantation.

"Can you give me something to prevent a woman from having babies?" Mary asked.

"Why, yes. If you're sure that's what you want."

"It's for me and my little sister. She's twelve. We don't want to have babies to be sold off like animals."

"Shouldn't that be your sister's decision?" Annie May asked.

"Do you have children, Annie May?"

"Fourteen."

"Do you know where they are?"

There was a long pause as the woman pondered the question.

"You provided your master with fourteen slaves to sell and exploit. I'm sure you had daughters. Did you want them to go through the same things you did? If you had a choice, would you have had those children?"

Annie May slowly shook her head. "No, honey. I wouldn't have."

"Neither do I or my sister."

"You can pass as white. Move East."

"If I have a black baby, how could I explain that to a white husband?"

The woman nodded. "I can give you something."

"Does it work? Are you sure it works?"

"It works," Annie May assured Mary.

"Is it an herb? Like what you inserted into me?"

"No. You drink it."

"That's better."

The old woman went into the house and came out with two small paper bags of white powder. "Dissolve this in a liquid. Just put it in a cup and drink it with anything except milk. Take it all at once. Stir it well. It's less than a fourth of a cup. Take it after you stop bleeding."

"Will it cause any pain?"

"No. None. I usually charge five dollars for it, but since I've already treated you, it's free."

Mary put ten dollars in the woman's hand. "I can pay." It felt good to know that neither she or her sister would contribute to populating the slaves in America.

John returned and picked Mary up, exactly as he said he would. She felt relieved when she saw him. John was a nice man who held a special place in her heart.

"You all right, Mary?" He stood as she walked down the steps. "You need some help up?"

"No, I'm fine. Thank you so much," she said. "Annie May would like to meet Hattie May. She thinks they're sisters."

"Spitting image," John confirmed, helping the old lady into the wagon. "I didn't want to be the one to bring it up," he said to Mary. "Get her hopes up. So few of us know our kin." John turned the wagon around. Then he said, "We need your help, Mary. You left us money, but we don't know how to count. Having trouble buying things, being black and all."

"I can help with that. When we get home, we'll take a

look and see what you all need. The authorities will write Mrs. Thatcher's children after the fever breaks."

"We're afraid they're going to sell the place—and us," John said.

"Ask Mrs. Thatcher's children to set you all free. They may grant it. Then go East or to Canada."

"Mary, I wouldn't know what to do as a free man. What if I can't find a job? How will I live? I'll need traveling money. Don't know how to read or write. We'll never say anything, but some of us have heard you reading to Mrs. Thatcher."

"I'll help you. Don't worry. If you get your freedom, I can get you out of the South."

"How are you going to do that? How can you get us out when you can't leave?"

"I'm leaving soon."

"You can get us out of here, Mary?"

"Yes, I can. All three of you."

He flashed a broad smile. "I'm going to hold you to that."

Annie May sat in the wagon between Mary and John. People didn't think much, seeing a white woman riding on a wagon with slaves.

When they reached Mrs. Thatcher's house, they all walked right through the front door. Mary went to Hattie May's room and gently shook her awake.

"There's someone downstairs to see you, Hattie May."

The old woman opened tired, red eyes and stared at her. "Someone to see me?"

"Maybe a relative of yours," Mary said.

Hattie May's face lit up like a lamp. She hurriedly got out of bed. Wearing nothing but her nightgown, she followed Mary down the stairs. At the bottom, she met Annie May. "My eyes must be playing a trick on me. Annie May, is that you?"

"What was your mother's name?" Annie May asked.

"Mabel," Hattie May replied without a second of hesitation.

They both cried and hugged each other for dear life.

"After all these years, we're together again," Annie May said. "How have you been, Hattie May?"

"Tired. They worked me to death over the years. Don't have much strength."

"Come live with me. I ain't got much, just an old shack in the swamps, but I make lots of money, more than I can ever use."

"When did you get your freedom?" Hattie May asked.

"Never did. They got the idea I was too old to work and too old to sell, so they turned me loose to fend for myself. I found this abandoned shack out there in the swamps and moved in. The government owns the land."

"You look real good, Annie May. Not worn down like me."

"I fooled my owners." Annie May laughed. "I got around a lot better than they thought I could. I'd pretend my joints hurt. I complained about how my back ached. If they told me to pick up something, I couldn't lift it. A man hit me a couple of times with a whip, and I fell to the ground and just lay there, moaning. I bent one of my arms sideways and walked with a limp, just like a cripple. They had their driver take me out in the middle of the swamps and turn me loose, as if I were a stray cat no one wanted. Guess they thought the gators would eat me. I'll tell you the whole story one day. I understand you need a place to live."

"Yes," Hattie May said. "I can't do much work. The only reason Mrs. Thatcher kept me around is that she felt sorry for me. With her gone, I have to go too."

"What plantation did you live at, Annie May?" John asked.

"I was at the Crawford's place," she said.

"That's only about twenty miles from here." John shook his head. "All these years, you two were living so close to each other."

"Sad, isn't it?" Hattie May placed her face in her palms and wept.

"Get your things together. Come home with me," Annie May insisted.

Hattie May looked down at herself. "I'm standing here, looking like a fool in my nightgown. Let me get dressed. I wonder if Mrs. Thatcher would mind if I took a few of her clothes."

"I doubt if she'd mind," Mary said.

"Just don't take nothing expensive. You don't want the law after you," Annie May said. She went upstairs to help her sister pack.

John looked around the room. "This is the life, isn't it? They live like kings, while we live like animals."

Mary was shocked. "You've never been in here?"

"Never. Mrs. Thatcher didn't treat us the way she treated you, Mary."

"I thought she treated you all better than Master Boyd treated his slaves."

"We were just slaves, Mary."

The sisters came downstairs, carrying two bags of things.

Hattie May said, "I overheard your conversation. Mrs. Thatcher was a nice lady. Still, we were only slaves to her."

Now Mary understood. Her master, Mrs. Thatcher, and Mr. Charles treated her differently—better—just because she didn't look black like the other slaves.

"I'll make us some lemonade," Mary said. She could hear the two old ladies chatting about everything they could think of as she made their drinks.

Mary returned to the living room with three glasses on a tray.

They sat in the grand living room, drinking lemonade and eating strawberry cake—something they couldn't have done in the presence of white folks.

"What do you do every day, John?" Annie May asked.

"Nothing. Not a worry in the world. Go where I want to go, when I want to go."

"I spend most of my time in my room," Hattie May said. "Have for two years."

***

Then Mary sat down next to Annie May. The woman took Mary's hands in hers. "You're a very nice girl, but I wouldn't want to cross you. You have an evil side. I see blood on your hands, child. Four times."

Mary jerked her hands back. Her stomach lurched. How could she have known?

"You'll never seek your final destination," Annie May said. "You shall remain here in the South forever."

Annie May took Mary by the hands a second time and read her palms. "I see death—death at a young age for you."

Mary quickly withdrew her hands from Annie May's grip. This time she stood and placed her hands behind her back. "You have no right to say those things to me," she growled. The old woman was a witch, and Mary wanted her out of Mrs. Thatcher's house.

"Your future can be altered," Annie May continued, her weathered eyes serious. "Let me help you. I can make your dreams come true. I have strong medicine that can help straighten things out for you."

"I'll help you with your things, Hattie May," Mary said, ignoring what Annie May had said. With hateful eyes on her, Mary headed toward the door. She had survived yellow jack, and she couldn't stand to hear Annie May say she was going to die.

Mary helped Hattie May into the wagon and said

goodbye. As Annie May climbed up, Mary had second thoughts and said, "Thanks for helping me out, Annie May. I know you mean well, but you're wrong about me."

"You know where I live. We can fix things. Visit me soon. I won't charge you a thing. You're welcome anytime. We'd love to have your company."

"Take care of Hattie May. Thanks again." She wasn't angry with the old woman anymore and managed a sincere smile. "Do you have your pass, John?"

"Mrs. Thatcher gave me one. Carry it everywhere I go. It has my name on it and who I work for."

Mary watched the wagon disappear from sight.

CHAPTER 14

THE CRAWFORD'S

A HUSKY MAN of about thirty stopped his wagon in the front yard of Mrs. Thatcher's house. He was probably a driver, but he didn't look anything like John or Josh. Mary had been sitting on the porch enjoying the cool morning breeze.

"You Mary?" the man asked.

"Yes," she replied, standing to get a better look at him.

"I'm a driver for the Crawford plantation. Four members of the family are deathly ill. You're needed there. Mr. Crawford and his sister died from yellow jack a month ago. The rest of the family is pretty sick."

"They have their own help. Why me?"

"That decision came straight from Master Boyd, Mary. I rightly don't know."

"Let me get a clean dress," she said.

Mary returned, carrying a canvas bag. She sat in the

wagon next to the driver, and the horse trotted away. An assortment of fruits and vegetables filled the back of the wagon.

"You just came from the fields?" she asked.

"Yes. I need to drop these things off at the hospital on my way through town," he said. "Shouldn't take long."

"Do you mind stopping by my place for a few minutes? It's on the way."

"I don't see any harm in that."

The two were silent as the wagon bounced along the road.

"Turn here," Mary said. "The house is back there."

"You got a house all to yourself?"

"With my family," she said.

"You're one lucky woman. I don't know my family."

Mary jumped down from the wagon, carrying one of the sacks of medicine she'd purchased from Annie May. As she suspected, only her sister and her youngest brother were home.

"Mary." Her sister hugged her. "Are you here to stay?"

"No. I'm in a hurry." Mary rushed into the kitchen, dumped the white powder into a cup, filled it with water, and stirred it until it all dissolved. "Drink this."

"What's it for, Mary?"

"It keeps you from having babies. You don't want babies, do you?"

Her sister frowned as she drank the contents of the cup. "It's nasty."

"It's a secret, like how I taught you to read and write. Never tell anyone. Not even Mama and Daddy."

"I haven't told yet."

"That's a good girl. I can't explain it to you now, but you don't want to have babies that the master can sell off like calves. If a man ever touches you inappropriately," Mary pointed, "down there, kick or dig your fingers in his private parts between his legs. Remember that?"

"Yes, Mary."

Mary rushed out the door. "Don't tell anyone I've been here."

"Bye, Mary."

As Mary and the driver entered New Orleans, the streets were empty. It was not the same place she'd remembered from only two months ago. It was eerie.

Before they reached the hospital, the stench of death permeated the area. Mary knew the odor of yellow jack victims, and she hated it. The staff had all the windows open to keep the place cool.

The driver backed his wagon up to the back door and set the brakes. He climbed down and banged on the door. Three black men exited the building and helped the driver unload the wagon. The driver got back into his seat and drove off. "I hate coming to this place," he said. "No matter how you go in, you always come out in a box."

There were two wagons parked near the rear, and two men had loaded several bodies into them.

The ride was about twenty miles from Mrs. Thatcher's

place, and it took them almost the remainder of the day to reach their final destination. The Crawford's house was a typical mansion, built from the sweat and blood of slaves. Mary pictured Annie May there, all crippled and being whipped.

When Mary knocked on the front door, the maid answered. The woman stared at her in disbelief.

"You Mary?" the woman asked.

"Yes. I was sent here to help."

"Come on in," the maid said.

Mary entered a living room that contained many windows, and lush green plants were everywhere. The walls were gray, and a piano stood tucked away in one corner. Two divans and some tables filled the room. She saw a huge crystal chandelier hanging from the ceiling, and cabinets full of dishes and wine bottles near the open dining room.

"Two of us help came down with yellow jack," the woman said. "I didn't think we could catch it. Usually only white folks die from it. They say you've done a lot of work with the sick and never caught it."

"So far," Mary said.

"We have four people upstairs sick with the fever. Mrs. Crawford, her two children, and her mother. There ain't nobody left here to take care of the place. Do you know how to read?"

"A little," Mary admitted.

"We need to buy groceries and things," the woman said. "Do you know how to do them things?"

"I do," Mary replied. "If money is available."

"I know where the money is. Can't touch it though."

"I can take care of that," Mary said.

"Come on upstairs. That's where they are."

Mary followed the woman to the top of the stairs. The layout of the house was similar to Mrs. Thatcher's. She sighed. Not all of their money and luxury could prevent them from dying. Yet she didn't feel sorry for them, not one bit, because of the way they used black folks like people used horses.

"This is Mrs. Crawford's bedroom." The door squeaked open, and Mary saw a middle-aged woman lying in bed. Her moaning stopped abruptly, and she vomited foul, black bile down the front of a beautiful green gown that matched her eyes. She had probably purchased her elegant wear from New York City.

"Can she speak?" Mary knew if she did, she would be incoherent.

"A little. The doctor left her some medicine, but she mostly throws it up."

"How long has she been sick?" Mary asked.

"Four days. Bad sick the last three," the woman said.

"Only the medicine can ease her pain until she dies," Mary said. "I can't do anything here. I'm not a doctor."

"They just want us to help keep them comfortable."

"I'll do my best," Mary said.

"Let's go down the hall," the woman said.

"This is little Sarah's room," the woman said as she opened the door. "She's seventeen but small for her age."

The woman was right. Sarah was about the size of Mary's twelve-year-old sister. She coughed up blood but never opened her eyes.

The room was pink, and a mirror covered half of one wall. The open closet revealed beautiful dresses and numerous pairs of shoes. Hairpins and ribbons covered the table at the girl's bedside. Tucked underneath the covers, she looked like a sleeping child.

The woman moved to the next door. "This is their oldest son. The youngest one lives in Chicago, but he's not allowed to visit, although he has tried several times." The boy lay on his side with his back to the door.

The woman escorted Mary to the last door, where an elderly woman lay in bed. She stared at them when they entered. Her condition was not as severe as the others.

"Who's this?" the old woman asked.

"This is Mary. She's from another plantation. Here to lend a hand, since the other help got sick."

"Why would a white woman be here?"

"I try to help all people," Mary said. "Can I get you anything?"

"Just some company. Someone white to talk to. My name is Barbra Atkins."

Mary took a seat next to the woman.

The housemaid said, "I'll leave you two alone."

Mary held the sick woman's hand.

"It's nice to see a white face. I know I'm dying. Will you write things down for me?" she asked Mary. "There's a pen and paper on the desk. Ink's in the first drawer."

Mary collected the items and used a book as a writing pad.

"I think maybe we're being punished for the way we treat these African people," she stated.

"Do you want me to write this down?" Mary asked.

"No," the woman said. "I want you to write my last will and testament, and letters to my other two daughters. At least they are safely away from this deathly place. Write my will first."

"I'm ready," Mary said.

"I have a house in Chicago, free and clear. My youngest daughter lives in it. I want her to have the house. She's a schoolteacher. Never married. I guess you can call her an old maid. Her name is Mary, like yours. Mary Ann Atkins is her name. I have money in the bank, and I'm part owner of this plantation. I'd like to leave my daughter's equal shares. My other daughter's name is Lois Neil Harper. She has three kids. One's on his way to becoming a doctor. The other two are worthless, but I guess every family has at least one like that. I own stocks in a shipping company in New York City. The owner was murdered right here in New Orleans two months ago.

"Well, let me see," she continued, "my personal things. I want everything in the house to go to my daughter, Mary Ann, since she already lives there. She takes good care of my things, like silver, china, and jewelry. She's smart, that one. Smart enough not to get married to a womanizing scum like her sister did. She's sick and dying, down the hall. Her husband moved out of her bedroom and slept with all the wenches, he did. There was nothing my daughter could do about it."

Mary wrote the woman's will and read it back to her.

"Would you like to read it?" Mary asked.

"Did you write it exactly as I dictated?"

"Yes."

"No, let me sign it." Blood from the woman's nose covered her hands, leaving bloody fingerprints on the page.

"I know we can't send mail out. Keep the will here in the house for safekeeping. This fever won't last forever. It hit Savanna, Georgia in 1820. Wasn't nearly as bad though."

"I'll leave it right here in your bedroom," Mary said.

"Now, my letters. When can you write them?" the woman asked.

"Whenever you're ready."

"I have a painful ache in my back, arms, and legs. I don't want to die, especially in such a miserable way. I've always thought I'd die in my sleep. I think I'll take a nap first. Come back later, honey."

Meanwhile, Mary paid the bills, purchased groceries, and balanced the books for the plantation. She was shocked and appalled at how much the owner had made in the past from slave labor. Mary never dreamed that plantations made so much money. Now the crops rotted in the fields, because they couldn't be shipped anywhere. Owners could only keep cotton if they had a place to store it. Master Boyd had a warehouse; perhaps the other plantation masters did as well.

Mary never got a chance to write the woman's letters, since the frail woman fell into a state of deliria and never recovered. Her skin didn't turn yellow like the other fever victims but remained a raw, bloody red. She died three days later, after Sarah and her brother. Somehow, Mrs. Crawford held on for another day.

CHAPTER 15

THE SEARCH FOR ANNIE MAY

ANOTHER DEVASTATING STORM hit New Orleans. Homes and businesses were destroyed, and people lost their livelihoods. The rain finally relented after two days of flooding. When the Crawford's driver took Mary back to Mrs. Thatcher's plantation, she went in search of John. He was bored and didn't mind driving Mary to Annie May's place. The woman was always on Mary's mind. She couldn't block out the words the woman said.

She'd ask the old woman to change her destiny.

What would it hurt?

Mary and John left early the next morning, arriving at Annie May's house about midday. The old place, now in rubble, had smashed in when it fell to the ground on one side.

"She must still be in there," Mary said to John. "Annie May."

John stepped down from the wagon quickly and investigated. The front door stood open. He walked up to it and peered inside. "Nobody's in here, Mary. I see an alligator. This house is in ruins. No one can live in here."

Mary asked in desperation, "Do you have any idea where she could have gone?"

"No," he said. "I'll ask around."

Maybe she didn't live through the storm. She wouldn't have been the only one.

***

The next job Master Boyd volunteered Mary for was at the hospital in New Orleans. The foul stench of yellow fever victims had fully engulfed the surrounding streets. Their soiled clothes and linens, and even the air that escaped their sickrooms met her before she'd entered the building. It was worse than the death camp. Patients lay in beds, some on the floor. She had to walk through black puke and blood and step over victims every couple of feet.

She stopped at the nurse's desk. "I'm Mary. I was asked to help out around here," she said to a woman carrying a bottle of laudanum in haste.

"You a nurse? You look kind of young."

"I've had some experience."

"Check all the patients. Have the dead and near dead driven to the death island. We need the space."

"Shouldn't the doctor determine who's dead and who's alive?"

"We don't have enough doctors left."

Mary trotted down the hall behind the nurse, almost running to keep up with her pace.

"Check their condition. Point out the critical ones, and let the boys take them out of here."

Mary stopped following the woman and started checking patients' vital signs. The nurse was right. Many were dead and others were near death.

The entire hospital was in chaos. Nurses and doctors had become sick and were soon patients themselves. Mary asked the slaves to load the wagons and rode with a convoy of the dead and dying to the death island. After helping get patients set up in tents, she rode back to the hospital.

Is this how Annie May predict my death?

Mary was sitting in the back of the hospital, taking a break, when she questioned one of the drivers. "Hello. Do you know a woman named Annie May?" she asked.

"Sure do. How are you, ma'am?"

She gazed around the death chamber. "Not bad under the circumstances."

"You a nurse?" he asked.

"Yes, from back East," Mary said. No one at the hospital knew she was black. Even the staff treated her as if she were white.

"Do you know where I can find Annie May? She has moved from the swamps."

"Rumors," he said. "Heard she went East with a sister of hers she found after many years apart."

"Hattie May," Mary said.

"Don't know her name. I reckon she made lots of money telling people's fortunes. Can you imagine that? Two slaves, too old to work and too old to sell. Who's going to question their freedom?"

"You sure she went East?"

"Can't be sure. Other people have been asking for her as well."

Mary never saw Annie May or Hattie May again.

***

Most of Mary's days were spent giving patients laudanum, which they usually threw up. She wrote wills and letters and collected more jewelry.

Then she met a black woman with the fever. She was lying on the floor in a storage room.

"What's your name, honey?" Mary asked.

"I don't want to die like this," the patient said. "Even in death, I'm separated from the white folks. They tell me about heaven and hell: I'm living in hell, and when I die, I'm staying in hell. I was once dumb enough to believe in that garbage."

"Where are your folks?"

"I'm a slave. Got no folks."

Mary spent all of her free time with the woman. She felt worse for her than anyone else, even Mrs. Thatcher.

One day, when Mary entered the storage room, the patient was sitting with her back pressed against the wall. "I feel better."

The patient's improvement was unusual for fever victims.

"You look better. Want something to eat?"

"No," the woman said. "Just some water."

Mary brought her a glass of water from the kitchen, and her patient gulped it all down.

"Thanks for helping me. Spending time with me. You're the nicest white lady I've ever met."

"All people should be treated the same," Mary said. "It'll be nice if you try to eat something. I can bring you some food."

"Not hungry."

She told Mary about her pitiful life—nothing different from other slaves.

Mary had never witnessed a yellow jack fever victim recover from the illness, and she hoped this woman would be the first. But three days later, she died.

Mary had a difficult time eating in the hospital. She had no choice but to consume whatever they served within the walls of the facility. Like most workers, she sat outside at a distance and ate. Everything had the smell of death, and food was becoming scarce, because nothing entered or left New Orleans. The only booming business in the city was undertaking.

Except for the sick and dying, the streets were empty.

Only Mary's work kept her mind off her own death. She was terrified and didn't want to die like her patients. *This must be the way Annie May have predicted I would perish.*

CHAPTER 16

MASTER BOYD

AFTER MARY HAD spent six days at the hospital, Josh showed up and waited for her outside. She had strict orders to report to the big house. Master Boyd and his wife were sick with the fever.

Mary hadn't been inside the grand mansion since the age of eleven. She showed up at the back door of the house in layers of filth from the hospital. She hadn't bathed in days, and the servant refused to allow her inside.

"Hello, Mary," the maid said. "You need to go to the creek and wash before you can come inside. Wait here; I'll get you a towel." The woman followed Mary to the creek, carrying a towel and a sheet.

"We heard that Mrs. Thatcher died from yellow jack, and now Master Boyd and his wife have contracted the disease," the housemaid said. "I've heard that you worked at the death camp and didn't catch it."

"So far, not yet," Mary admitted.

"The only thing people talk about around here is the fever. No one works the fields anymore."

"What do the slaves do all day?"

"Just sit around playing games. It's bad for white folks, but the slaves are glad they don't have to work. They take turns caring for the livestock until the cotton is ready to pick."

"Are they going to put the cotton in the warehouse?" Mary asked.

"That's what I heard. Vegetables are rotting in the fields, Mary."

"I know," Mary said. "Same thing at all the other plantations."

When they reached the creek, Mary stripped and waded into the shallow end of the water. The housemaid gave her a bar of lye soap, and she scrubbed her hair and body. When Mary stepped out of the water, the head overseer was standing there, watching her.

"My, ain't you beautiful all over."

The maid quickly wrapped the sheet around Mary. "You ain't got no business peeking at women," she said to the man.

"I peek at any slave I want. Have anyone I want too," he said.

"You better not let Master Boyd hear you say that," the woman said.

He flashed a sly smile. "He and the missus are dying.

I have a feeling that things are going to change around here once Becky takes over. No more preferential treatment for you, Mary."

Mary tugged the sheet tightly around her body and walked away barefoot. "I'm needed at the house."

"You can't do nothing for them. You save any of those folks at the death camp?" he asked.

She took a good look at him. "That's the way it starts: pale skin, red eyes, and aching muscles. You do have those symptoms, don't you?" Mary asked.

His eyes bulged. "What are you saying?"

"You have the fever, mister," Mary hissed. "So, get off your high horse. You're going to the death camp."

"I just have a cold, that's all."

"We'll see in a couple of days." Mary walked off, leaving the astounded overseer at the creek to think about his own death.

When they arrived at the big house, the maid asked Mary to wait in her bedroom until she found clothes and shoes for her to wear. Mary dressed but kept her wet hair tied up in a towel.

"Where is Becky?" Mary asked.

"In her room. She refuses to leave it, even to eat. Our job is to help take care of the sick. It's bad. The doctor was here yesterday but didn't tell me anything. Just gave me laudanum and said to keep them comfortable. Follow me. I'll take you to them."

Mary climbed the wide mahogany staircase to a room

of luxury the slaves had provided for Master Boyd. The hardwood floor creaked as she stepped into the bedroom, then the thick rug on the floor muffled her footsteps. Everything was white: the four-poster bed and its covers, the furniture, and even the rug. The window curtains were open, and the room was bright, but the stench of death was strong in the air. She didn't need to be a doctor to know that Master Boyd didn't have long to live. His skin had turned yellow. Each time his weak lungs gasped for air, blood dripped from his nose and covered the front of his pajamas. His feverish blue eyes searched the ceiling.

Mary was glad to know that the death wagon would take him away and dump him into an unmarked grave like the savage animal he was. He was her father, yet she hated him. He'd taken advantage of her mother and other black women over the years, even young girls.

His wife lay in bed next to him and closest to Mary, still coherent but extremely pale and thin. She gazed up at Mary from red eyes with dark circles around them, making her look like a raccoon. She didn't speak, just turned her head and stared at the ceiling.

Master Boyd died that night, but they took his body to the cemetery rather than to the death island. Mary sat at his wife's side for five days until she passed. Becky laid her to rest in the cemetery next to her father. The white overseer died as well. *Did he think he was invincible?*

Mrs. Thatcher wasn't taken to the cemetery, because

no one had claimed her remains. Maybe that's why the woman told the doctor Mary was her next of kin. If Mary had known at the time, she would have claimed the woman's remains and made sure she had a proper burial.

***

As the temperature decreased, so did the number of yellow jack victims. By late September, New Orleans was back to normal.

So was Mary's life.

One day she noticed that the slaves had built a stand in front of the big house. It was a mystery to everyone. Rumor was it was an auction block for the sale of slaves. It was a four-foot square that stood about a foot off the ground.

Becky had taken control of the plantation. She said her father had been too generous to the slaves and kept more than he needed. The remaining ones would just have to work harder.

Chairs sat in front of the stand for the crowd of people that had gathered. Becky sat near the back as the auction started. She wore a blue dress the color of her eyes with a matching bonnet. Buyers sat in the audience and chit-chatted until the bidding began.

Mary stood a distance from the auction block with her mother. They held each other and cried. The night before, the overseers had separated Mary's three siblings from the rest of her family. They would be sold, and Becky didn't want them to have any more contact with their family members.

The new white overseer stood on the stand in the morning light and called out, "I'm the overseer for this entire plantation, and I'll be auctioning off slaves today on behalf of Miss Becky Boyd."

Becky stood and curtseyed.

"She's so young," a voice rolled from the audience.

"We'd like to thank you, folks, for taking the journey to view the stock we have here today. If anyone has a question, just raise your hand, but I prefer you use that hand to place a bid."

Dry laughter erupted from the crowd.

"Let's get started," the auctioneer said. "First, we have the finest of our bucks."

A brawny slave, well over six feet tall, stood on the auction block, shirtless. His huge muscles bulged like melons. "This buck is twenty-eight years old. There's still lots of work left in him. He can pick up one end of a wagon while you change the wheel. Let's start the bidding at nine-fifty. Do I hear more?"

"A thousand." A man in the audience raised his hand.

"A thousand-fifty," a woman countered.

"Eleven," her competitor announced.

"Eleven-fifty," the woman responded.

"Do I hear twelve? Come on, folks. He can work harder than two slaves can. Do I hear twelve?"

Silence.

"Going once. Going twice. Sold to Mrs. Cora Lee for eleven hundred and fifty dollars."

Everyone clapped, and Mrs. Cora Lee bowed her head and flashed a graceful smile.

***

Cyris was up next. The auctioneer motioned him to step right up onto the stand.

The overseer said, "We have a seventeen-year-old here. He has many years of service left in him. A hard worker who doesn't need anyone on his back. Let's start the bid at seven hundred dollars."

A hand shot up. "Seven," a bidder with long black hair said.

There were no more takers.

"Come on, folks, we're talking about a strapping young buck here."

"Have him remove his shirt," the bidder requested.

"Take off your shirt, boy," the auctioneer commanded.

Cyris did as instructed.

"Now have him turn around," the man said.

As Cyris turned around, he heard moans from the crowd of buyers.

"He has been whipped," a man gasped.

"Do I hear seven-fifty?" the auctioneer asked.

"I'm revoking my offer," the bidder said. "Why was he

whipped if he's such a great slave? If Aetna finds out he's been whipped, the company might not insure him for full price."

"I don't know," the overseer said. He turned and looked at Miss Becky.

"Lower the bid to six hundred," she said.

"Five," the man who had made the original bid offered.

The auctioneer looked at Becky again, and she nodded her approval.

"Sold to this gentleman for five hundred dollars."

The man stood and introduced himself. "I'm Ron Johnston from Kentucky. We know how to keep our slaves in line. I won't have any problems with this one."

"These asking prices are mighty high," a voice from the audience complained. "I've traveled a long distance. Took the stage here because of promised bargain prices. I can buy slaves for these prices back home."

"That's right," voices from the crowd said.

***

Mary's sister was up for sale next. Mary wanted to hug her and tell her everything would be all right. However, she knew it wasn't so. Tears flowed down Mary's cheeks. She curled her hand into a fist and bit down on her index and middle fingers. Mary wished she were the one up for sale. Her little sister had not been exposed to what other young black girls her age had. She hadn't a clue about men, sex, and rape.

"This wench is only twelve. She can have many healthy babies in the future. Another hard worker," the man said.

"Do I hear five hundred?"

"Five," a man from the crowd said. "How do we know if she can even produce babies?"

"I'll find out," the man from Kentucky said. "Five-fifty."

Mary's mother ran to Becky's side and dropped to her knees. "Please, don't sell my daughter."

Becky smiled and said, "Get her out of here."

Two slaves dragged Mary's mother away. "You have to go ... before you're whipped," one said.

A balding master with blond hair stepped onto the auction block. "Six hundred." He touched the young girl's shoulders, then his hands went to her small breasts and stopped between her legs. "I like 'em young. Six hundred," he repeated. The man smiled.

Mary didn't know where her mother got a pair of scissors from, but she rushed onto the auction block and stabbed the buyer between his legs several times before anyone could intervene. Screaming out, he grabbed his bloody genitals and went down in pain.

"You're not touching my child," her mother hissed.

Becky jumped from her chair. "Hang her. Hang her now."

Three black overseers dragged Mary's mother to a nearby tree and threw a rope over a thick branch.

"Stop. Don't do this to me." Then she screamed, "Go East, Mary." She struggled as the men forced her onto a chair and pulled a noose snug around her neck.

"Mama." Mary ran toward her mother, but the men held her back. She fought against the strongholds on her arm and waist without avail. "Let me go. Mama."

Her mother had attacked the wrong person. She should have stabbed and killed Becky. Mary wanted to but didn't have a knife.

One of the men tied the loose end to a branch and kicked the chair out from underneath Mary's mother. It all happened so fast. Mary's life had changed within a matter of minutes. She clasped her hands over her mouth and watched in horror while her mother twitched and squirmed. Then she turned her head and wept. She hated Becky.

Mary threw up, forever scarred by what she'd just witnessed—a pain far worse than a whip could ever inflict.

"Someone get this man to a doctor," the auctioneer yelled.

The injured master lay on the platform in a fetal position, holding his bloody genitals. Two of the slaves put him into a wagon and drove off.

After the crowd settled down, Becky stood. "I'm sorry for what happened. I have taken care of the problem. I—"

"What kind of plantation are you running here? Allowing a slave to attack a white man." Mrs. Cora Lee yelled, jumping to her feet. "Why, I don't feel safe here." She pointed a stiff finger at the big slave she'd just purchased. "I'm not buying him. He could do lots of damage

before someone kills him. I won't have him on my plantation, threatening our lives."

"Mrs. Cora Lee—" Becky said.

The woman rushed away. "Where is my driver?"

Other outbursts occurred throughout the group as
well.

The auctioneer cleared his throat and tried to calm
the crowd. "Now, folks, we've had a bit of a problem here.
The troublemaker is hanging right there. The man is on
his way to the doctor. There's nothing more we can do."
With Mary's mother hanging by her neck in the background, he said, "Let's continue with the auction."

Mary dropped to her knees. The surrounding crowd
prevented her from seeing her mother's body swinging
from the rope. Two of the black women took Mary by the
arms and tried to lead her away, but she was determined
to stay.

"The last bid for this young wench was five hundred
and fifty. Do I hear six?"

Silence.

"Five-fifty, going once. Going twice. Sold to the gentleman from Kentucky for five hundred and fifty dollars."

The man from Kentucky raised his hand. "I change
my bid to four hundred."

Becky sold Mary's sister off to a plantation owner
from Kentucky for four hundred dollars. Mary didn't
know what would happen to Iris. For the first time in her
little sister's life, she'd know what being a slave meant.

Mary felt worthless, helpless. She could do nothing to save her siblings. She knew then and there she would have to survive in an evil world where there was no justice.

***

As the auction continued. Cyris stood between Mary's sister and the big, brawny slave. The next person on the auction block was an elderly woman. The crowd erupted into laughter.

She had white hair and leaned forward with a hump in her back.

"Quiet down," the auctioneer said. "Now, I know she's up there in age, but she's a good maid and a good cook. Quiet," he said to the still-amused crowd. "Do I hear two hundred?"

The crowd roared again.

"I'll take her if you pay me four hundred," the man from Kentucky yelled.

"She's too old to work. She can't have babies. No one is going to purchase her," a voice from the crowd added.

"All right, one hundred," the auctioneer said. "Do I hear one hundred?"

"I'll have to buy another slave to help her out of bed every morning," a voice shouted.

The crowd exploded into laughter again.

No one purchased the old woman. Cyris never knew what owners did with slaves who could no longer work.

He'd heard rumors that the masters put them down as they did horses that were no longer useful.

***

Mary watched as the huge black man stood on the auction block again.

"Folks. This buck is a steal. Eleven-fifty was the last bid. His offspring will be just as large as him. "Do I hear twelve hundred?"

Silence.

"Do I hear eleven-fifty?"

The man from Kentucky said, "Seven hundred."

"Seven hundred. Do I hear eight?"

"Seven-fifty," a young man said.

"Seven-fifty. Do I hear eight?"

Silence.

"Seven-fifty. Going once. Going twice. Sold for seven hundred and fifty dollars to this young man."

Next, the auctioneer stood Mary's three-year-old brother on the stand.

"Mama," he yelled. "I want my Mama. Where is my daddy?"

He saw Mary and climbed down from the auction block. "Mary." He held out his arms like a baby who wanted her to pick him up. "Come get me, Mary."

Several men restrained Mary. She could hear the fear

and confusion in her little brother's voice, but she could do nothing to help him, to comfort him.

The auctioneer placed Mary's little brother back on the auction block and placed a hand on the boy's back. "This is a yearling, just turned three. An owner can teach him many things within the next two years—how to serve at parties, fetch things. Let's start the bid at five hundred dollars."

Silence.

"Think the price is too high? How about four-fifty? Any takers?"

"I'll pay four hundred. Not a penny more," a plantation master said.

"Sold for four hundred dollars."

Mary's oldest brother was up for sale next. She realized Becky was deliberately separating her family.

"Take your shirt off, boy." The auctioneer gazed into the crowd. "Now turn around. He's eight years old. A fine worker. Do I hear six hundred dollars?"

Silence.

"Six hundred," the auctioneer said again. "Any takers? He's a bargain. How about five-fifty?"

"Five-fifty," another man from the crowd offered.

"Going once, going twice. Sold for five hundred and fifty dollars."

Since different masters had purchased Mary's brothers, they would never see each other again—and she would never see either of them.

Becky stood and said, "I'm closing this auction. I realize that I've had a problem here today, but I'm not going to sit by and give away my slaves."

***

Mary and Walter later attended her mother's burial. However, her siblings weren't allowed. It wasn't a funeral like the ones the white people had. They just dumped her body into a hole in the ground and covered it—no marker. After all, she was just an animal to them.

***

Mrs. Thatcher's children returned to their old homestead and put the place up for sale.

Mary visited them, but she didn't tell Mrs. Thatcher's son who his real father was. They treated her like a guest. She sat in the living room, ate cookies, and drank tea with them. Neither brought their children.

Mary gave Mrs. Thatcher's daughter, Diane, all the jewelry and letters she'd collected during her stay at the death camp and the hospital. Diane said she'd turn them over to the sheriff's department, because they could easily find and identify the deceased's next of kin. Part of the collection was the necklace and wedding band Mrs. Thatcher had given Mary. Diane accepted the wedding ring but insisted Mary keep the necklace.

Diane said goodbye, telling Mary that her

mother-in-law had her kids, and she had to be getting back to the city. She ended up spending only a few days there before taking the eastbound coach. Her brother stayed on to take care of the estate sale.

CHAPTER 17

THE ROAD TO FREEDOM

LATE ONE AFTERNOON, all three of Mrs. Thatcher's old work hands came to Mary's house. Surprised to see the men, Mary walked out on the porch and greeted them.

"Hello, Mary," John said. "Good news. Mrs. Thatcher's children gave us our freedom. It's all legal for the three of us." He lowered his voice. "You said you can help us."

"Get your things together and pick me up here tomorrow morning. We're going to the stage depot. The best route is to take the stage to the nearest train station. Where are you all going?"

"From what you told us, Canada is the best place."

The two other men nodded.

"We don't have any traveling money," John said.

Mary whispered, "You'll have some tomorrow. Traveling money and enough to set up at your final destination."

John whispered back, "Where'll you get money from? We don't want to get hanged for stealing."

"It's not stolen money," Mary assured them.

***

The next morning, Mary took the men to the same mercantile where she'd tried on Becky's dress. The shopkeeper remembered her also from the time Mrs. Thatcher had purchased two dresses there for her. The three men walked through the back door while Mary walked through the front. "I need a traveling bag for each of these men and two sets of clothes," Mary said.

"What kind of clothes?" the shopkeeper asked. "Most of the menswear in here is for gentlemen."

"These men have been granted their freedom. They are now gentlemen."

The shopkeeper asked, "Do they know their sizes?"

Mary looked at them.

"No," John replied.

"Can't you measure them?"

"Sure," he said. "Step this way."

Two customers in the shop stared in disbelief, but the clerk ignored them. One left the store, while the other hung around watching.

"Where can they change?"

"Not in here. In the shed out back," the shopkeeper said, which seemed to please the onlooker.

"Guess we'll have to change in the shed," John said.

"The door is unlocked," the clerk said.

Mary's three friends walked out to the shed with new clothes, hats, shoes, and warm jackets to accommodate the colder Northern climate.

Mary waited outside until the three men had changed clothes.

"You look like gentlemen from the East," she said at first glance.

They grinned from ear to ear, and Mary was proud of them for wanting a better life. As they walked to the stage depot, citizens stared. Mary walked in front of them, entered the depot, and said, "I need three tickets to Detroit."

"Michigan?" the clerk asked.

An elderly woman gasped, "I can't believe you brought them in here."

Mary snapped at the woman, "This building doesn't have a back door. These men are traveling."

Mary turned her attention back to the man behind the counter. "Yes, Detroit, Michigan."

"The fastest route is to take the coach to the nearest train station."

Mary placed money on the counter. "How much for three tickets?"

"You'll have to purchase the train tickets at the rail station in Montgomery."

"That's fine. Three tickets to Montgomery."

"They got walking papers?" he asked.

"Show him your papers, men. Mrs. Thatcher's children freed them yesterday. It's all legal," she said proudly. The clerk studied the papers, looking skeptical, but sold her the tickets.

Mary had already given each man a wad of cash. She took them outside. "I know you don't know how to count. You don't need much money to buy food. Keep a few bills in your pocket, hide the rest at all times. When it comes to money, trust no one. Tell people you have only enough money for food."

"I'm afraid," one of the men said.

"We all are," John said.

"Try to stick together. Until you leave the South, sleep at the stage depot. If you have to spend the night somewhere up North, find a black family and stay with them. And don't let them know you're carrying money. Tell them you're poor men who just got your freedom. When you get to the train station, you'll have to purchase your own ticket to Detroit, then from Detroit to Canada. Actually, you can walk to Canada. It's less than half a mile. Try to learn how to count during your journey."

"Thank you, Mary," John whispered. "What are you going to do?"

"I'm out of here too. Goodbye, men. Have a safe trip."

"How can we ever repay you, Miss Mary?" John said aloud.

"Live a good life," she answered. "The life you deserve."

***

Mary watched them get into the midday stage bound for Montgomery. She then drove the team of horses to her own home and asked Josh to return them to Mrs. Thatcher's son. Although she'd never ridden a horse, she needed one to ride into town the next morning.

"Cyris, will you meet me at the creek tomorrow morning before dawn with a horse? I'm leaving here. This is the only thing I'll ever ask you to do for me."

"I'll have to sneak the horse out late tonight, Mary. Sometimes stable hands like to sleep in the hayloft rather than the crowded slave quarters. They usually get up pretty early."

"All right, tie off the horse at the creek where the log in the water is. I'll get him tonight."

"He'll be there."

"I'm counting on you, Cyris."

"I promise," he said. "Since I've been sold, I don't work anymore. I have lots of free time on my hands. Might go back to the creek real early and take one last swim before I leave."

"When are you leaving?" Mary asked.

"Don't know. They don't tell us anything. I thought we'd leave the day the man bought us. The master who purchased us has to figure out how to get us to Kentucky. I hear it's a long distance."

"But it's closer to Canada," Mary said. "Take care of my

sister the best you can. She's going to have a hard time adjusting. When I move to New York City, I'm going to buy you and her. I don't know who purchased my brothers."

"Ask around, Mary. You might find out."

"I have. Either no one knows, or they won't tell. I don't know what state they'll be in either."

"I'll take care of your sister, Mary. The best I can. But there's a limit."

"I know, Cyris. I know. One more thing … I don't know how to ride a horse."

"You've seen men mount. Do what you saw them do, just like you learned how to swim by watching Jimmy."

"You ever ride a horse?"

"No, but I know how to bridle and saddle one."

Mary went to the stables that afternoon and found a boy about her age, working alone.

From a distance, she watched him groom and ride a horse.

She heard a horse whinnying as she approached the area. "Can I ride?"

He turned around as if she'd startled him.

"Sure," he said, leading the horse into the barn. He turned around and scanned the area. "All right, climb on. You can mount him from either side, but most prefer the left side. Put your left foot in the stirrup, hold onto the saddle horn, and stand up while bringing your right foot over."

Mary got on the horse, and he gave her the reins.

"That's it. Keep both feet in the stirrups."

"How do I make it go?"

"Gently kick him in the side."

She did, and the horse started walking.

"If you want it to go left, you pull the left rein in that direction. Do the same thing if you want it to go right."

Mary rode the horse around in a circle right there in the barn.

"Get off now," he said. "I can't let anyone see you riding him."

Mary got off the horse. "Thank you. I've seen people ride, and it's as easy as it looks."

"I've seen you around. You're Mary," he said.

"Yes. I don't get out much."

"Why don't you come around and talk to me sometime?"

"We can talk now," Mary said.

One of the overseers saw Mary in the barn. "What are you doing in here, girl?"

"Just talking, that's all," Mary said.

"Don't you have a job to do? He does. Get back to work, Art."

"Bye, Art," Mary said, and rushed away from the evil-eyed overseer.

CHAPTER 18

REVENGE

THE HEAD OVERSEERS delivered orders to Mary directly from Becky. Other than going to the slave quarters to eat, she had to remain inside her house. She was never to go to the creek again or even sit in the yard. Mary was a prisoner in her own home.

When Becky finally summoned Mary to the big house, she entered the parlor and stood in front of her half-sister. Hate emanated from Mary like the rays from a July sun. She wanted to kill Becky, but her half-sister had a guard standing on either side. She wore a nice green dress with white lace around the neckline and sleeves. A white hat with green feathers crowned her head, as if she was about to take a trip.

"Becky. Why are these men here?"

"To protect me from you. After that crazy stunt your mother pulled, I wouldn't dare be left alone with you."

"You got that right," Mary said. "I'd kill you in a minute. Still might."

"I could have you whipped for threatening my life, even hanged. That no-account mother of yours ruined one of my customers for life. I'd have her dug up and hanged again if I thought it would help the situation. She ruined my auction."

Mary's voice was cold, distant. "You're responsible for murdering my mother."

"Well, Mary. As you've learned, things are going to be different around here from now on. I made sure I sold your sister to a plantation owner who likes little girls. So, her life will be miserable too. From now on, she'll learn how to work like a slave should."

Mary fantasized about standing over Becky's body, watching the life flee from it just as she'd watched Jimmy die—and she wanted to tell her so.

Becky held a teacup in her hand and sat with her head held high like a queen. "I have a new outfit for you to wear." She shoved a box in Mary's direction with her foot. "The dress, hat, and shoes are lovely. Picked them out myself. I want you looking your best. You're going on the auction block two days from now. Men as far away as Texas are coming to look at you. Can't have you standing in front of a crowd of men dressed in rags, can I? You should bring twenty times as much as those other black wenches. That's what you'll be, Mary, a wench. By the time men get through studding you, and the babies you'll have, you won't look so pretty anymore. I'm deliberately looking for a master who beats his wenches. Life is going to be pretty harsh for you from now on. A wench is all you'll ever be good for. You're not fit to empty my slop bucket. Now get out, you worthless whore." Becky crossed her legs and kicked out a foot. She took a sip of tea and smiled.

Fuming, Mary went home to an empty house. Walter, her stepfather, was the only one left in her family, and he was working in the fields. They had become closer since it was just the two of them left. Now, someone else would get their house, and he would move into the slave quarters.

Walter came home, exhausted—as usual.

"I'm getting too old to work this hard," he said.

"Men older than you work harder."

"They're used to it. Master Boyd did spoil us. Now I'll have to pay for it in sweat."

"I met with Becky today. She's going to sell me too."

He wasn't shocked but said, "Come here, girl."

They hugged for a long time before letting go.

"I'm going to kill Becky," Mary said.

"You can't get to her. No more talk like that."

"I've talked to the slaves who work in the big house. That old lady they tried to sell at the auction was their cook for years. She's dead now. The house workers believe Becky had her poisoned, because she threw up green puke before she died. They say Becky spends most of her time in her room these days—up most of the nights and sleeps in until noon."

"You'd never succeed, Mary, and they'd hang you just for talking about it. Look at what happened to your poor mother. I really loved her."

"I know … Daddy." This was the first time she had ever referred to Walter as her father, and she meant it. "We have to eat with the other slaves from now on. Food won't be delivered here anymore."

"Most of the food we had left is gone," he said. "I stopped at the quarters and grabbed some supper on my way home. You ate, Mary?"

"There's still some bacon left. I ate some of that."

"You need more than that in your stomach. I'm going to bed."

Mary stuffed everything worthwhile into her canvas bag, leaving a traveling dress out on the bed for a quick getaway. She could feel the excitement building as she thought about her escape.

That night, under total darkness, Mary opened the kitchen window of the big house and crawled through it. Only one woman slept in the house during the night, in case Becky needed something, and she was hard of hearing. Mary retrieved one of the large butcher knives from the kitchen and eased up the stairs. The steps creaked, so she walked on the sides rather than in the center. At the top of the stairs, her body was shaking—she was not as calm as she'd been when she killed her last tormentor.

This was the big fish—the most important one. She slowly eased open the door to Becky's bedroom and crept inside. Mary stopped and studied the room. The last time she'd been in Becky's room, it was painted and decorated in pink. Now everything was blue. An oil painting of her late mother hung on one wall.

Her target lay in bed on her back with her eyes closed. An open book lay at her side. The lamp on the nightstand gave off a faint glow. Mary slowly made her way to Becky's side, gripping the knife with both hands.

Mary raised the knife high in the air, and her half-sister's eyelids fluttered open. Becky opened her mouth to scream, but the blade penetrated the center of her chest, and the scream never escaped her lips.

"I killed Jimmy," Mary admitted. "I drowned that little water rat." Mary straddled Becky and repeatedly stabbed her until she was exhausted. Leaving the knife stuck in Becky's chest, Mary blew out the lamp and closed the door on her way out. With her heart thumping and her body shaking, Mary rushed back home, washed up, and put on one of her finest dresses. Careful not to wake Walter, she took the travel bag containing the wardrobe and hat Mrs. Thatcher had given her.

***

Cyris had already picked out the horse and placed him in the front stall away from the hayloft. He eased open the barn door and entered. Snores serenaded from above him. Placing the saddle on the horse, he led it out the open door and quietly closed it behind him. He secured the saddle and led the horse toward the creek in total darkness. He didn't light a lantern until he was near the willows. Walking to the designated place, Cyris stopped the horse under a pine tree and tied the reins to a low-hanging branch so Mary could reach them.

***

Mary grabbed a lantern but didn't light it. She ran past her mother's burial site and to the creek as fast as possible. Once she reached the willows, everything was pitch black. As she neared the bank of the creek, she lit the lantern and kept the flame low, just bright enough to see where she stepped. She saw another light coming toward her. She blew out her lantern and froze in her steps. Then she saw the horse and Cyris. He had tied it exactly where he said he would.

"Cyris, is that you?" she whispered.

"Mary."

"Your lantern is glowing too bright. Turn it down," she warned.

He turned the wick down as he approached her. "You leaving now?"

"Yes, I have to be in town to catch the next stage or ship. They both leave at about six."

He gazed at the bag in her hand. "You going to New York City, Mary?"

"Don't know. I'm headed that way. I just want to get out of the South."

"Good luck, Mary," he said, hugging her.

She patted him on the back. "Good luck to you, Cyris. You'd better get out of here. Turn that lantern off once you leave this wooded area."

"I will. Bye, Mary." He took off, smiling, feeling that Mary would now have a bright future for herself.

They went in opposite directions, Mary toward her stash of cash and Cyris toward his slave quarters.

Mary dropped her bag near the horse and waded through grass and small weeds until she reached her hiding place. Removing the top from the stump, she took the metal box containing the cash she'd been collecting. Returning to the horse, she hooked her travel bag on the saddle.

By the time the housekeeper discovered Becky's body, Mary would be miles away. They would expect her to head east, which is why she would travel north up the Mississippi River to St. Louis. The authorities wouldn't expect her to have money or the ability to read and write. It would take months for the news to reach all over the states, and they had no photo of her, just a description. In addition, she looked too white to pass as half-black.

Breathing heavily from excitement, she attempted to untie the reins and release the horse. Just then, a snake bit her three times on the neck before she even knew it was there, wrapped around the branch. A fearful, wretched scream echoed throughout the woods. Knowing she needed to get help fast, she picked up the box and ran. Suddenly she felt light-headed. She stumbled and fell face up. Her eyelids fluttered toward the starlit sky. She had trouble breathing then her world went black.

***

Cyris hadn't made it back to the slave quarters when he heard the scream. "Mary," he said.

He rushed back toward the creek, his heart pounding out of control. Master Jimmy had drowned there, and two others had died there as well. *Was Mary another victim?* When he approached her, she was lying flat on her back with the lantern at her side. Her vacant eyes stared unblinkingly at the sky. He saw the bites on her neck and knew they were undoubtedly from a snake. When he'd been twelve years old, he had seen a snake bite a slave on the neck, and the man had quickly died. There were three bite marks on Mary's neck. He dropped to his knees and checked her pulse. No pulse, no heartbeat.

She was dead.

He moved her fingers from around the handle of the box, one by one. Looking inside, he found a treasure trove. His heart thumped even faster, and he froze in place for a long time. Looking around, he saw no one else.

Where did Mary get so much money? Had she stolen it? He forced the lid closed on the box stuffed with cash, ran to a tree, placed the box on the opposite side, and covered it with leaves and branches. No, he thought. He might be leaving in the morning and wouldn't be able to return and retrieve the money. So, he stuffed his pockets full—some bulged from under his shirt, even in his socks. He picked up the lantern and ran back toward his quarters, blowing out the flame after he'd left the creek. When he reached his quarters, he sneaked into his room, hid the money in his sack, and slid into bed, but he couldn't sleep. Mary was dead, and he couldn't tell a soul.

Cyris waited until midday and walked to the creek. Mary's body was still there, as well as the horse, tied to a branch. Cyris pretended to be in shock when he ran back to his quarters and alerted the others.

"It's Mary." he yelled to the nearest overseer. "I think she's dead."

"Where is she?" the man asked.

"At the creek," Cyris stated.

The man stood. "Another murder at the creek," he said to the other men. "Someone get the sheriff. Lead the way, boy."

A crowd of black and white overseers followed Cyris back to Mary's body.

"What's this horse doing here?" one man asked.

They examined Mary's body. "Look at the bite marks on her neck."

"Bet it was a moccasin," someone said.

They all concluded that Mary had died from snake-bites. But what was she doing at the creek with a horse? Running away, folks concluded, because Becky had planned to sell her.

This was the fourth death at the creek, and it was now off limits.

Then, the group turned to Cyris. "What were you doing here?"

"I walk here sometimes."

"You've been sold. Got no business leaving your quarters," one of the overseers snapped.

"I didn't think it would hurt to take a walk," Cyris said.

"Maybe you killed those other people as well."

The thought had never occurred to Cyris. "I've never killed nobody."

"She was bitten by a snake, not murdered," a man said. "The boy was with me all day when Mr. Charles was killed. It was on a Sunday, his day off. I remember it well."

"How did she get a horse out here without someone seeing her?"

***

Later that day, the sheriff and the doctor showed up. Mary's death was officially ruled an accident. There were many questions and few answers.

The slaves started digging a hole in the ground next to Mary's mother and planned to bury her there.

Then a ruckus broke out at the big house. The maid had found Miss Becky's body in her bedroom.

"Murdered," was all they said.

The doctor and sheriff rushed in to investigate.

"Mary must have killed Becky," one of the overseers said. "I was standing in the parlor with Becky when she gave Mary the news about selling her, and I heard Mary say she would kill Becky for having her mother hanged."

"Did you notice anything different about the house this morning?" the sheriff asked the maid.

"The kitchen window was open when I came downstairs."

"Let's take a look," the sheriff said.

"I already closed the window," the woman said.

"I want to see those kitchen knives. Any missing?" the sheriff asked.

"Yes, suh," the maid wept. "The one I found sticking in poor Miss Becky's chest belongs in the kitchen."

"Where did Mary live?" the sheriff asked one of the overseers. "I'd like to see her room."

"I'll take you there." The overseer led the way.

***

Mary's house was empty. Her stepfather was working in the fields. The sheriff searched the place and found Mary's bloodstained clothes. "She was the killer, all right. Get her father back here. I want to talk to him."

While Josh and an overseer went to pick up Walter, the sheriff went back to the big house. The doctor had written the death certificate for Becky and said there was nothing more he could do. He'd send the undertaker back to collect her body.

When Walter returned home, the sheriff was waiting for him outside. "Mary's dead," the sheriff said. "Bitten by a snake. A boy found her body about noon today at the creek. She died last night, attempting to run away."

"Last night," Walter cried. "I thought she was in her room."

"How come you didn't miss her?"

"She was here when I got home late yesterday. I get up early in the morning. We don't cook here anymore, so I went to the quarters, ate breakfast, and then went straight to work. I didn't see her this morning." Tears welled up in his eyes. "She was the last relative I had left."

"She murdered Becky last night."

Mary's father was shocked. "What?"

"Stabbed her to death while she slept."

He thought about Mary planning to kill Becky. "She wouldn't do that. Can you prove she did it?"

"I have two witnesses who overheard Mary threatening to kill Becky," the sheriff said. "Her bloody clothes are still back there in her bedroom. Did you help her do it? Becky had your wife hanged. Sold off all your children. You had motives."

"No," Walter said.

"I don't believe she pulled this thing off all by herself. Someone gave her a horse to get away on. You used to work at the stables. She didn't go there in the middle of the night and get a horse all by herself."

"I don't know anything about it," Walter said, nervously looking around at the crowd that had gathered. "If she did do it, I didn't help her. You got to believe me."

***

Cyris stood in the center of the crowd. He knew they were going to hang Walter no matter what he claimed. They needed someone to pay for Becky's death. Mary was already dead, so they were going to use Walter as an example.

"You're what we call a co-conspirator," the sheriff said to Walter. "Get a rope."

"No," Walter pleaded. Tears rolled down his cheeks. "I didn't do it." He gazed into the distance and muttered, "Mary, girl, I always said you'd get me hanged one day."

The sheriff shouted, "Does anyone here know anything about the horse? About Mary running away? Did anyone hear anything last night?"

At first, he only saw blank faces in the crowd of slaves.

"When I had to go last night, I saw a light at the creek," a man said.

"And you didn't say anything?" the overseer asked.

"Didn't know I was supposed to," the man answered.

"Was it early or late last night?"

"Late, about midnight, maybe early this morning. Can't say for sure."

The sheriff threw a rope over one of the branches of the tree that Mary used to sit under. "Put the noose around his neck."

Overseers always carried around nooses to threaten slaves if they got out of order.

"Stop," the head overseer said. "Hanging is too good for him. Hold his arm over this block."

The men did as instructed.

The overseer used a nearby ax and chopped off Walter's hand. Walter cried out in pain as blood squirted from his severed wrist.

"Get that other arm up here, boys," the overseer demanded.

The men held the struggling Walter's arm on the block. It took three blows before the overseer severed it. A deathly scream echoed across the land.

"Get me some lamp oil," the overseer said.

A slave entered the house and came out with a gallon jug of oil. As Walter lay on the ground, bleeding to death, the overseer doused him with oil, then set him afire.

Walter let out a continuous, deathly scream. His body twitched as he yelled and moaned.

The slaves watched through horrified eyes. Some cried, others held their breath, and many turned their heads from the scene.

Cyris couldn't watch anymore. He cried for Mary and her innocent father.

Before the flames went out, the overseer said, "Now hang him."

He looked at the sheriff and said, "This is what happens when masters treat slaves like white folks."

If they had known that Cyris had led the horse to the creek, he knew he would have received the same punishment as Walter.

"Don't Mr. Boyd have sons from his first marriage?" the sheriff then asked.

"One's someplace out West," the overseer said. "The family hasn't heard from him in over ten years. I heard he and his father had a bad fight. He vowed never to return here." He leaned in and whispered, "He fell in love with one of the slaves. Wanted to free them all."

The sheriff chuckled. "The other son?"

"Went out to sea. His ship hasn't been found yet. Believed to be dead."

"I'm going to have to find his only surviving son. What's his name, and where do you think he is?"

"Allan Boyd, somewhere in Oregon."

***

During most of the night, the memory of deathly screams and the stench of burning flesh kept Cyris awake. When he did fall asleep, he dreamed about the money he had, and he hoped no one would find it. Then it occurred to him that he would be leaving the plantation any day now, and his new owner might have him searched. His only hiding place was in his sack with the few rags he owned. If they found the money, the overseers would hang him as well.

Someone shook Cyris awake. It was time to head for his new plantation. He collected his sack and marched out into the night. Mary's father was still hanging from the tree when Cyris left the Boyd plantation for good.

Cyris didn't see Mary's sister until he fell in line with slaves from other plantations, but most were as black as night and didn't speak English.

**

Slave trading from Africa had ended years earlier, but somehow, according to Mary, they still came into America. Shackles bound their wrists, and leg irons clinked around their ankles. This was the third time he'd met slaves who didn't speak English.

His personal contents were in a sack thrown over his shoulder. Slaves never stole each other's belongings because they all possessed the same thing—nothing. Cyris didn't know what his new life would be like, but it couldn't possibly be worse than his old one.

A convoy of wagons, consisting of over a hundred slaves and twelve overseers, headed toward Kentucky during the middle of the night. He knew Kentucky was up north, closer to Canada, so Cyris didn't mind making the trip. He and Mary's sister were the only two from his plantation to join the group bound for Kentucky. Cyris didn't know the few slaves there from nearby plantations.

CHAPTER 19

IRIS

IRIS WAS AMONG the slaves on the trip to Kentucky, and she was frightened to death. She'd watched her mother's hanging and stood helpless as her brothers were sold. In addition, men had ripped her from Mary's arms the previous night and placed her on the auction block. Why hadn't her father rescued her, taken her into his arms, and told her everything would be all right? *Where is he?*

"Your name is Cyris, isn't it?" Iris asked. "You're my sister's friend. Her only friend."

"Yes. Mary was my friend."

"You don't want to be her friend anymore?" Iris asked.

He didn't have the heart to tell her that Mary and her father were dead.

"We've been sold to another plantation. We won't see Mary again," Cyris said.

"I'll never see Mary again?" Iris cried out.

"We've been sold. Don't you know what that means?"

"No," she cried. "Where are they taking us?"

"We're slaves, Iris. They're going to force us to work hard, all day long, for the rest of our lives."

"I know other girls worked, but I never did."

"That's going to change, Iris. You lived as if you were free. You have to work now."

"Doing what?"

"Whatever white folks tell you to do, or you'll be whipped like Mary," he admitted.

"Why hasn't my daddy come for me?"

"He can't, Iris. He's just a slave. You don't belong to him anymore. You belong to the man who bought you. He paid money for you, and he ain't going to let you go until he works you to death. After that, you won't be good for nothing."

"What are we going to do, Cyris?"

"Do what they tell us to do. Stop crying. No one is going to help you. They took me from my mother when I was younger than you are. At least you got a chance to be with your mother, remember her, and know what she looks like."

"Mary taught me how to read, Cyris. I couldn't tell my parents. Mary taught me lots of things."

"She didn't teach you enough, Iris. Not nearly enough."

Cyris was right. Mary didn't teach Iris things she needed to know. Cyris explained to her about men and women, where babies came from, and why masters expected her to have many babies they could sell.

"I can't have babies, Cyris. My sister gave me medicine, so I can't."

He smiled. "That's Mary, thinking of everything."

"I'm tired of walking. My feet and legs are so sore."

"We'll have our turn to ride," he said. "You have to keep up with the wagons. Before we make it to Kentucky, your body will get used to it."

Their light New Orleans clothes didn't accommodate the colder climate. They slept on the cold ground with three under one blanket. Iris was so relieved to see the sun, she cried.

When not on guard duty, the white overseers slept in the wagons.

"Why did we stop traveling at night?" Iris asked. "We are warmer when we walk nights and sleep during the day."

"Don't know. We're a long way from New Orleans now. Maybe that's why."

All day and night, the overseers stood over them with guns.

Riding on the wagon with Cyris, Iris asked, "What kind of plantation are these other people from? They speak and dress strange. I don't think they understand each other."

"Africa," Cyris said. "Didn't Mary tell you about Africa? That's where we all came from."

"Why are they wearing chains?"

"They just got off a ship, and white folks are afraid of them. The strongest and most determined ones will be whipped, tortured, or killed to make an example for the rest. That's the only way they know how to control us."

"I've tried talking with them, but they know not a word of English."

"They'll learn. Won't be allowed to speak their own language or worship their own religion."

"Watch your talk, boy," a slave from another plantation said.

"The overseers are not close enough to hear us, and these people don't speak English. Who's going to tell what I say except you?"

"You think they're taking all of us to the same plantation?" Iris asked.

"I doubt it," he said. "They'll sell some of us to surrounding farms."

"I want to stay with you, Cyris."

"Mary said it's colder in Kentucky," he said. "It snows there."

Late that night, Iris heard a gunshot that woke everyone up. A guard had gunned down a slave in chains who had attempted to escape. Iris didn't sleep for the remainder of the night.

The slaves received two meals per day—breakfast and supper. Iris helped women from another plantation cook breakfast for the group. Before they started the convoy that morning, the overseers removed the chains from the dead slave and left his body along the roadside.

***

Later that day, four men approached the convoy, and it came to a halt.

"I can see most are right off the boat," one of the men said. "How much are you asking? They have to be taught to heed and work, so the price can't be that high."

"How much?" another man asked. "We can make a deal."

The guards shunned them and moved on, saying they couldn't make a sale.

When the weather became too harsh, the slaves couldn't bear the cold. The guards gave them light jackets to wear. At least they could stick their hands in their pockets to keep them warm.

"I can keep you warm, girl," one of the guards said to Iris.

"No," she said. "If you touch me, I'll tell my new master."

"Come here, little girl." He grabbed her by her arm, pulled her to a wagon, and threw her into the back.

Mary had told her where to attack a man if he tried to touch her inappropriately. She kicked him between his legs and ran back into the group. When he recovered, he removed his belt and beat her.

***

In the middle of the night, Cyris heard Iris screaming for help from one of the wagons. If he intervened, the guards would kill him. The screaming stopped, but Cyris couldn't go back to sleep.

The next morning, Iris helped with the cooking, still loudly crying. Cyris couldn't and didn't know how to console her. No one could, not even Mary. The girl had learned what it was like to be a real slave.

For the duration of the trip, Iris slept in the back of a wagon. She never talked to Cyris about it, and he didn't ask. No one did.

He couldn't count the days it took them to reach the great state of Kentucky. Each night, the temperature dropped lower than the night before, but they didn't get any more blankets to keep themselves warm.

CHAPTER 20

RUNNING AWAY

WHEN CYRIS REACHED the new plantation, stars were fading from sight and morning was near. Overseers herded them into a camp like cattle into a slaughterhouse.

They cracked their whips and yelled in booming voices, "Inside, you wretched devils. Make room in here."

The group slowly moved along, but Cyris saw the chance to slip away with his sack of goods, and he did. He ran faster than ever, following the North Star. He wished Iris could've joined him, but she'd only slow him down, and the guards would miss her before they'd miss him. Due to the number of slaves, it might take days, if they ever missed him at all.

He ran day and night, mostly off the main roads, begging for food here and there, and taking on a few odd jobs for meals. After three weeks on the trail, exhaustion and hunger made him stop. He was now in Ohio. About dusk, he stumbled into a wagon camp where a man and a woman sat around a fire.

"Excuse me, folks." He shook in fear as he entered their camp. "Do you have some food to spare?"

"Yes," the woman said kindly. "Just finished supper. Have some leftover stew and bread."

"I'm mighty grateful. Except for a few apples, I haven't had a meal in two days," Cyris said.

He gulped down the cold stew and stale bread, and it tasted so good.

"Where did you come from?" the man asked.

"New Orleans," Cyris said between chewing.

"Are you free or a slave?" the woman asked.

"Free. Looking for my father. He's headed to Montana."

He could have eaten more, but that was all they had left.

"We're meeting up with a wagon train in a few weeks," the man said. "My name is Mr. Adam, and this is my wife, Mrs. Sally. Lucky you. We're on our way to the Montana Territory too, if the Indians permit us to get that far." Cyris had simply picked a state, not knowing where Montana was or the difference between Montana and the Montana Territory.

"My name is Cyris."

"Cyrus," the man chuckled. "After the Greek, meaning lord and master."

"My name is Cy-ris," he repeated.

"Never heard that name before. What does it mean?"

"Don't rightly know. Just a name. Can I walk behind your wagon, suh?"

"You can ride with us," Mrs. Sally said. "You look mighty young. How old are you?"

"Eighteen, next month," Cyris said, hearing a baby crying inside the wagon.

Mrs. Sally smiled. "That noise is our three-month-old son, Christopher."

"He has a mighty strong voice, ma'am," Cyris said.

The woman had blonde hair, same as Mary's but not as thick and pretty. She was a thin, pale woman with a kind, gentle face.

"You can travel with us if you don't mind sleeping under the wagon," Mr. Adam said. "You can work for your keep."

"I've slept in worse places," Cyris admitted.

***

Cyris was cold, and Mr. Adam gave him one of his old jackets. He had been traveling with the couple for about a week, and he felt comfortable with them. His rear end was sore from riding in the wagon all day, and he wondered how they could have stood it all the way from back East. The old wagon rattled, bounced, and shook all the time. If he were milk, he would have turned into butter the first day.

Mrs. Sally taught him how to write his name and read

a little. He took care of the horses and provided wood for the fire. Mrs. Sally's cooking wasn't that good unless you liked everything overcooked or burned, so Cyris took over cooking and washing the dishes as well. The couple liked having him around, doing all their chores, just like back on the master's plantation.

He'd thought about asking Mr. Adam to teach him how to shoot.

The man had left his rifle leaning against the wagon wheel one morning. Cyris picked it up and admired its power. He aimed it at a tree but didn't squeeze the trigger. When Mr. Adam walked around the wagon, he yelled, "What are you doing with your black hands on my rifle."

Cyris stuttered, "Wh-why, I was just holding it. It looks like a nice gun. I didn't mean nothing by it. Honest, I didn't."

Mr. Adam snatched the gun from Cyris and shoved him hard against the side of the wagon. "Never touch my gun again. You hear?"

"Yes, suh." Cyris's voice trembled in fear. He thought the man was going to strike him. "I won't touch it again."

"What's all the shouting about?" Mrs. Sally asked, climbing from the back of the wagon.

"This boy was holding my rifle," Mr. Adam blurted out.

Mrs. Sally gasped, "What?" She stared at Cyris. "Why would you do such a foolish thing?"

They acted as if he'd threatened to kill them with it.

"Let's get moving," Mr. Adam said. He placed his gun beside him on the front seat, and Mrs. Sally climbed up to join him.

Cyris took his sack from the back of the wagon and just stood there.

"You coming, boy?" Mr. Adam asked.

Cyris smiled and jumped up on the seat next to Mrs. Sally, just as he'd done during most of the trip, and threw his sack into the back of the wagon. He knew he needed to leave them, perhaps during the middle of the night. He was safer traveling with them for now, but he didn't trust them.

***

A few days later, they met a regiment of soldiers, whose jobs were to scout the trails, protecting white people from Indian savages. Cyris feared the Indians more than he did the whites. At least white people wouldn't take his scalp.

"Where are you folks headed?" a soldier with three stripes on each sleeves asked, bringing his horse and the regiment to a halt and creating a storm of dust.

"We're hooking up with a wagon train bounded for the Montana Territory," Mr. Adam said.

"That's not a safe place to be right now. The Indians are killing settlers out there. This trail is not so safe either.

War parties are on the prowl. We scout this area, but redskins could be anywhere."

"My sister wrote us a letter. They have problems sometimes, but she says it's not that bad."

"When is the last time you heard from her?" the soldier asked.

"About six months ago," Mrs. Sally said. "We won't reach Montana Territory until next summer."

"I can't make you folks turn around, but I advise it. Who's he?" The soldier nodded at Cyris.

"A boy we brought along to help us with our chores," Mr. Adam said.

"If you picked him up along the way, he might be a runaway slave."

"No. He's been with us since we left home," Mrs. Sally said. "He didn't have a place to stay, so we took him in."

"Where are you from, boy?" the soldier asked.

"Back East," Cyris said. He couldn't remember the state.

"You're from the South. He's a runaway, isn't he?"

"He's ours now. We didn't mean to lie to you, but he really needs a place to live. He can help us around the farm once we get settled," Mr. Adam said.

"We don't plan to force him to remain with us," Mrs. Sally said, "unless he wants to."

"I have Indians to worry about, not runaway slaves. You folks be careful. Good day." The soldier tipped his hat. "Ma'am."

The soldiers rode off, carrying a storm of dust with them.

"Maybe we should turn around," Mrs. Sally said to her husband.

"Nonsense. When we join up with the wagon train, there'll be men who can shoot as well as I can. We can protect ourselves. No redskins are keeping us from a new start."

"The soldier frightened me," Mrs. Sally said. "For all we know, my sister and her family could be dead by now. After all, it's been six months since we've heard from them."

"There were only twenty-two soldiers in that company. There'll be more men in our wagon train than that. Don't worry, dear. We'll be fine."

"I've heard about what the Indians do to white women. They take white children too—and raise them as savages like themselves." She glanced at Cyris. "I can't imagine what they'd do to you."

Cyris cringed, frightened out of his mind. He'd escaped being a slave only to be massacred by red devils. If he returned to the plantation, they'd hang him for sure. Either way, he was doomed to death. So, he had to take his chances on living as a free man.

"That's why I want to learn how to shoot, Mr. Adam."

"Get that out of your mind, boy. You don't need to know how to shoot—and never touch another man's gun."

"I thought if the Indians attacked, I could use one of the guns in the back of the wagon to help you. Two shooters are better than one."

"How do you know about my extra guns?" Mr. Adam snapped.

"I told him," Mrs. Sally said. "Didn't think it would hurt."

"Don't you ever touch any of my guns again, boy. You hear me?"

"Yes, suh, Mr. Adam."

"We're running out of meat. Do you know how to snare a rabbit, Cyris?"

"No, suh. Why don't you just shoot one?"

"Gunfire will alert the Indians. Didn't they teach you nothing on that plantation, boy?"

"How to plant, pick cotton, gather vegetables, hoe, and mind my own business."

"You trying to get smart with me?" Mr. Adam yelled. "How would you like to have your black ass left out here in the middle of nowhere to starve, or to face the red-skins all on your own? Those heathens won't be so nice to you, I promise. You think they'd take you in, feed you, treat you nice, and provide you with a place to stay? After they take that kinky hair of yours, they're going to torture you slowly and painfully. Before they get through with you, you'll be begging them to finish you off."

Cyris had seen Mary's father chopped up and set ablaze by white men.

Could the Indians be any worse?

"I wasn't trying to be smart. That's just the way things were. We slaughtered cows, chickens, and pigs. We didn't have to hunt for them. We knew exactly where they were."

"Don't pay Mr. Adam no mind." Mrs. Sally took her husband by his arm and smiled. "We won't dare leave you out here alone."

"Don't bet on it," Mr. Adam said.

"Can I drive the team sometimes?" Cyris asked.

"No, you can't. I thought they taught you how to mind your own damned business on that plantation."

Mr. Adam was pushing the horses too hard. They ate beef jerky and cold biscuits for lunch, never stopping to rest the animals. If they came across a watering hole, he'd only stop long enough for the horses to drink. When they made camp at night, he'd stake them out and let them graze.

"I can count to a hundred," Cyris said to Mrs. Sally. "Been practicing reading too."

"Sally, you shouldn't teach him things like that."

"It won't hurt anything, Adam," she said. "Besides, it's practice for my becoming a school teacher. I've written all of my lesson plans, and I'm using them on Cyris. I have to teach children and adults how to read and write."

"They don't have a school there yet."

She placed an arm around her husband's shoulder and leaned in. "My sister said they're building a school come summer. We can help."

"We'll see," Mr. Adam said.

**

They had been on the trail for weeks. In about another week, they'd hook up with the wagon train and spend the winter months in a small town. During noon meals, Cyris had been saving beef jerky, because he planned to take off on his own any day soon. Nobody questioned a black boy traveling with a white couple. He was so far from Kentucky, no one would think of looking for him in Indiana. Why, he had hidden in plain sight.

Mrs. Sally seemed friendly enough, but he had doubts about Mr. Adam.

"We've saved enough money to put down on a small farm near my sister and her husband's place in the Montana Territory," Mrs. Sally said while sitting around a campfire. "We can't pay you anything, but you can sleep in the barn and work for your keep."

Cyris had heard that all his life. They'd made plans for him for when they reached Montana. He would sleep in the barn with the animals and be their own personal slave. "Thanks, but I'll be looking for my father."

The couple made eye contact. They knew he was a runaway slave looking for passage north to Canada.

"We hope you'll change your mind," Mrs. Sally said.

Cyris and Mr. Adam unhooked the horses and got ready to bed down for the night.

Mrs. Sally took out the dishes and cookware while Cyris threw more wood on the fire.

"Take off that shirt. Let me mend your sleeve," Mrs. Sally offered.

"No, thank you," Cyris said.

"You can have one of Adam's old shirts. It might be a little big for you," she pressed.

"I have another one," Cyris said.

"Take off that shirt, boy," Mr. Adam demanded.

Cyris unbuttoned his shirt and slipped out of it. "It's kind of dirty, ma'am."

Mrs. Sally gasped, "What happened to your back, Cyris?"

"Some people didn't like things I said."

Since he had his shirt off, Cyris washed in the nearby stream and slipped into a clean shirt. When he walked back to the wagon, both the man and his wife were holding fistfuls of his paper money.

"Where did you get all this money from, Cyris? Robbed a bank?" Mrs. Sally asked.

"That's my money," Cyris said. "I found it."

"Why, ain't you the lucky one? Money just rains out of the sky on you," Mr. Adam said.

"How many white people did you murder to get this much money?" Mrs. Sally asked, thumbing through her handful. "There must be thousands here. We could buy twenty—a hundred—farms with this."

Mr. Adam held a handful of beef jerky. "You've been hoarding food, too. Planned to run away, didn't you?" Then he pulled out a watch and necklace with his free hand. "Watch ain't worth nothing—but look at the size of this diamond. Is that why you got all those whip marks on your back, boy? You sure fooled us."

The greed on their faces frightened Cyris. "Put my things back." He dashed for his bag, but Mr. Adam dropped his loot and punched Cyris in the stomach.

Cyris doubled over from the blow and went down on one knee.

Mrs. Sally said, "You're nothing but a stinking thief."

The pain in Cyris's stomach almost crippled him. When he went for his money again, Mrs. Sally tossed her husband his rifle, and he caught it in midair.

"Get out of our camp, or I'll blow you away," Mr. Adam said.

"Not without my money," Cyris said.

He pointed his rifle at Cyris. "You're not getting this money back. So, move along, boy."

Mr. Adam was a full-grown man, big with rugged strength. Cyris hesitated, then sprung another attack. "You're not keeping my money."

Cyris saw a muzzle flash. The rifle boomed, then a burning pain shot through his side. Shrieking, he tried to stem the flow of blood from his wound. As he lay there on the ground, the couple picked up the money and stuffed it back into the sack.

Would he die like Mary, staring up at the sky?

Mr. Adam started hitching up the team. "Let's move to another site," he said.

"You can't leave me here," Cyris gasped.

Mrs. Sally started loading the wagon.

"Please, don't leave me here to die," Cyris begged.

With the team hitched and the wagon loaded, Mr. Adam jumped into the driver's seat with his wife. An arrow penetrated his chest. Then there was lots of hooting and hollering. Mrs. Sally screamed. Christopher cried.

Cyris's world went black, and everything around him faded into silence.

Chapter 21

Indian Village

WHEN CYRIS AWOKE, he saw glowing embers from the firepit in the center of a tipi. A bandage covered his wound. An Indian boy sat at his side curiously running his fingers through Cyris's hair.

His side was so sore, he couldn't move. A man with long, raven hair pushed back the entrance flap and walked inside the tipi. He was wearing Mr. Adam's coat and hat. He stared down at Cyris for a few seconds, then turned and stalked out. Shortly after, a woman came in and fed him warm, bitter tea from a cup.

Cyris had heard that the Indians were red devils. But their skin wasn't red, as the white people said, but brown like his.

After the woman left, he lay there and observed his surroundings. Little Christopher lay sleeping on a blanket on the other side of him. Attached to a tipi pole was

Mrs. Sally's hair. It still had the pink ribbon tied in it. Cyris's pulse raced, keeping up with the vibration of fear throughout his body. Were they keeping him alive just to torture him in the future?

He fell asleep.

***

A week passed before Cyris could sit up on his own. The Indians fed him well, except some of it was hard to keep down. Before long, he could walk through the village all on his own. They were all interested in his hair. The people weren't savages like the white people claimed. They were normal folks who were fighting to protect their land. Like the slaves right off the ships from Africa, there was a language barrier, so they used hand signs to communicate until he could learn their language.

One of the men held the watch that was in the bag with his money. Cyris asked him where he got it. The man took him to another tipi, where he found the bag with his raggedy clothes and all of his money. The big diamond necklace was gone.

The Indians wanted him to stay with them, but he had to be moving on. He asked if he could take Christopher back to his own people, but the man refused. The boy was safe here, he was told. All the women fussed over him.

Winter was upon them, and the Indians wouldn't

allow him to leave. They said he couldn't travel through the snow, and the cold would be too unbearable. So Cyris remained there as the winter howled down from the Northland. The Indians taught him how to make his own tipi. The women gathered wood and buffalo chips for fire. He didn't have a woman, so he gathered his own. The Indians were right: he would have frozen to death if he'd kept going on foot. Cyris studied the Indian language and within a month had mastered most of the major words. He, in turn, taught them English—the best he knew how. They didn't use complete sentences, just keywords that meant certain things.

It had gotten too chilly for a long-sleeved shirt, so the village pulled together and made him a buckskin jacket and some trousers. His shoes had holes in them, so they provided him with a pair of high-topped moccasins and leggings for the snowy season. Cyris enjoyed living with the Indians. He wasn't treated as a slave, or differently from everyone else. They accepted him as one of their own. They named him Sleeping Buffalo, because his hair resembled that of the buffalo and he'd slept for days after they'd found him.

***

White Antelope, the younger of the chief's two surviving sons, was skinny and tall. The tribe respected him, not just because he was the chief's son, but because of his courage and bravery. White Antelope had killed more buffaloes than any other brave had. He was a furious fighter against the white man. He was known as the brave who had killed Mr. Adam and wore his clothes as a trophy.

White Antelope and a big brave called Black Bear were Cyris's friends. Black Bear was the tallest and largest Indian in the village. He spoke in a gentle tone and was the champion fighter among the braves.

White Antelope and Black Bear were also Cyris's mentors.

"You need to learn how to become a great brave," White Antelope said one day. "Me and Black Bear," he said, pointing to the big brave, "will teach you our way of life, and how to hunt in order to survive."

"What do I need to do?" Cyris asked.

"Are you a good rider?" Black Bear asked.

"I've never ridden a horse," Cyris said.

"First, we teach you how to ride, hunt buffalo, how to fight," Black Bear said. He stood there, holding the reins of a horse. He threw a water pouch on the ground. "Take this horse into a gallop and pick it up."

How did they expect him to pick up the water pouch while riding on a horse? Without a saddle or a stirrup, he couldn't even get on the thing's back. He'd seen the Indians do it, so he ran up alongside the horse and tried to jump on its back, but his legs didn't reach, and he went crashing to the ground. A crowd had gathered, and everyone laughed. Cyris felt like an idiot. He led the horse to a pile of wood, walked up to the top, and slid onto the horse's back. The audience still laughed.

Cyris bounced up and down on the horse and said, "Get up, boy." The horse didn't move.

More laughter.

"Kick him in the side," Black Bear said.

Cyris gave the horse a hard kick, digging his heels into the animal's side. The animal took off with such speed Cyris fell backward, did a somersault, and landed on the ground—square on his butt. His pride was hurt more than anything else was. The crowd roared with laughter.

Cyris stood and brushed the dirt from his pants. White Antelope took another mount and went after the galloping horse. When he returned, everyone was still laughing.

White Antelope demonstrated how to mount the horse. After three tries, Cyris succeeded. He jumped as high as he could and straddled the horse. The crowd cheered. He felt a great relief in his shoulders.

White Antelope said, "Gently kick him in the side. The harder you kick him, the faster he'll run."

This time Cyris gently nudged the horse in its side, and it walked around the area. Using the reins, he made the animal turn from side to side. Everyone in the crowd smiled. He nudged the horse harder, and it galloped around in a circle. He ran the horse for a while, then tried to pick up the water pouch, but he fell off instead of completing his task. He repeatedly tried until he could retrieve the water pouch without falling from his horse. He did it three more times before White Antelope ended his day of training.

The next morning, Cyris did some extra training on his own. He became faster and more accurate—efficient. Within two days, he'd learned how to ride a horse Indian-style. He challenged the best brave in the village and won. His friends praised him for being such a fast learner.

The braves demonstrated how to make a bow and arrows from certain types of wood and flint rocks. He painted the tips of his shafts black and practiced until he got good at shooting it. Then he made a deerskin quiver for his arrows.

Young boys usually killed rabbits to keep the village in fresh meat during the winter, but Cyris didn't feel a bit disgraced for doing the task. He killed more rabbits than all the boys combined. His hardest challenge was galloping a horse while notching his bow and shooting a target with accuracy. He practiced continuously.

White Antelope and Black Bear taught him how to use a tomahawk. He didn't have his own, so he borrowed theirs. White Antelope demonstrated first. He threw the ax and drove it into a tree trunk. Next, Black Bear threw his ax, and it flipped through the air several times before lodging into a trunk. When Cyris threw the ax, the handle hit the tree and bounced off. He practiced for days before the ax finally penetrated the bark. He learned how to throw it hard enough to chop off small branches. Since there were not enough rifles for everyone, they didn't teach him how to shoot a gun.

***

The village scouts had located a herd of buffalo, which aroused eagerness within the tribe. That night, the men held a hunting ritual. They painted their faces and performed a vivid dance to bring about good fortune before their hunt. They said the greater the ritual, the greater their chance of killing buffalo. Cyris joined in, chanting and dancing around in a circle like a fool.

The warriors drew diagrams in the dirt, showing Cyris how they surrounded the buffalo herds and attacked, picking out only the largest male for the kill. They performed horseback maneuvers as well.

Tomorrow would be a great day for the Indians. They planned to kill buffaloes and collect enough meat to last them throughout the rest of the winter months. Cyris joined in their excitement and looked forward to the next day.

White Antelope woke Cyris in the early dawn. "Sleeping Buffalo, we hunt today. We'll teach you how to kill and skin buffalo."

Cyris exclaimed, "When do we leave?"

"Now. Only twelve of us are going. The rest will remain here to protect our village, in case the soldiers come."

Men and two boys, who were about ten years old, were ready to mount at the edge of the village. White Antelope and a few braves carried lances. They had a horse for Cyris with a water pouch and buffalo jerky.

The braves mounted and set out, leading ten pack-horses. They traveled most of the day before they spotted the herd.

White Antelope said, "Sleeping Buffalo, you and Black Bear come with me. Let's circle in this direction."

Cyris held his bow. Many arrows were in the quiver slung over his shoulders. He guessed the Indians lived as his ancestors did back in Africa, but he realized he didn't want to live like this, always hunting for food.

The three men remained together as the group surrounded the herd, hooting and hollering. The herd stampeded as the men galloped in closer, rushing the buffalo. The braves didn't use guns but bows and arrows, since gunfire might alert the soldiers to their location. The arrows were also preferred, because a hunter could easily claim the animal he'd killed by identifying his own arrow.

After a few missed attempts, Cyris shot an arrow and hit his target in the neck, and the huge, galloping male went down on its front knees. Cyris couldn't help feeling awed, and proud. After the herd moved on, they'd killed ten buffaloes. The Indians then leaped from their mounts and slit the throats of the beasts.

One of the buffaloes had White Antelope's lance thrust into its side. The braves didn't hang the animals up by their hind legs and skin them as the slaves did on the plantation. They sliced down the back to remove the hatched area and cut off the front legs and shoulder blades. The hump meat, innards, and ribs came next. Then the men severed the spine and removed the pelvis and hind legs. The neck and head came off as one part.

They cut up the meat, placed it back into the hide, and took it to their village. The brain and hump meat were delicacies among the Indian men. They all got a piece, even if it was a small piece. It had something to do with manhood and spirits.

To them, hunting was not a choice, but a way of life. Everyone in the village had to work in order to survive, and most of the Indians' diet came from the buffalo. They used every part of the beast. The hides would be used for sleeping rugs, because the hunt took place during the winter months when the buffalo had their massive winter coats. Hides for tipi coverings, bedding, clothes, moccasins, and robes came from hunts conducted in the early summer after the buffalo had shed their winter coats.

The tribe also made cups from hooves and horns, and they used sinew for sewing and making bowstrings. Bones were used to make knives, tools, or even glue (by boiling). The Indians used the buffalo hair for rope, pads, and halters. The women made pemmican, a mixture of berries, buffalo meat, and fat that would last the tribe throughout the winter months. Meat was dried and stretched to make jerky. The Indians also killed buck deer, and when the season was right, they killed the does as well. The women fried corn mush cakes throughout the winter.

Since one of Cyris's arrows brought down a buffalo, he had become a warrior among the braves. Now they looked up to him and treated him as a great tribe member.

That day of the hunt, even one of the ten-year-old boys had taken down a buffalo. His family was so proud of their son, now a brave as well.

***

Cyris's fire and sleeping robe kept him warm that night. He lay there thinking his life was great. He would have considered remaining with the Indians if he thought they had a chance against the enemy, but he knew white folk. For every white person the Indians killed, there would be ten more to take his place. The Indians were doomed. They wouldn't find justice in the world but would eventually be wiped out or used like his black brothers and sisters—used up, until nothing was left. Mary had told him about how the Indians had helped the white people when they first came to America. They would have never survived the winter if not for the Indians.

Now, the whites repaid them by taking their land and killing them.

America was supposed to be "the land of the free." But Cyris just couldn't see or accept this slogan, being a slave.

***

Cyris woke to a heavy frost that morning and something else. Soldiers as thick as a buffalo herd were swooping down on the village without warning.

"Long knives are here," a woman screamed.

A bullet hit her in the chest as Cyris exited his tipi. The baby in her arms took a bullet as well.

The soldiers gunned down everyone in sight. Men, women, and children fell dead or wounded in an instant. Women screamed, and children cried. As other braves did, Cyris grabbed his bow and arrow and started shooting at the enemies. He was good with his weapon, and each shot was a hit. If the soldiers found him killing white men, they would have tortured and hanged him for sure.

Braves with rifles shot soldiers. Each time a brave went down, another one picked up his gun and continued firing.

When the soldiers retreated, a fourth of the village was either dead or wounded. A few tipis were on fire, and little Christopher was gone.

Cyris counted about forty soldiers, wounded or dead. It didn't take long for the tribe to torture the wounded men to death, strip them of their possessions, and move their bodies to a desolate area for the animals to feed on.

The Indians recovered many guns and much ammunition from the fallen soldiers. They took their clothes, hats, and swords. They now had more guns, enough for each brave, and more horses. The tribe would still have to share tipis until they could rebuild.

They demonstrated to Cyris how to look down the sight of a rifle at his target, so he would shoot more accurately.

***

The village held a huge burial ceremony. Cyris didn't have to attend, but he wanted to learn about the Indian ways. The men chanted and women cried. They wrapped their dead in buffalo hides and took them to the ancient burial grounds. The burial chambers were on scaffolds about six feet off the ground. The relatives were laid to rest, while the tribe wished them safe travels into happy hunting grounds.

Viewing the ceremony, Cyris thought about how the Indians' ways made no sense. To him, their ways and beliefs seemed just like his experience with white people. They were always trying to convert slaves to their religion. God was good to white folks, but not to slaves or the Indians, or so it seemed to Cyris.

***

On the night of the first heavy snow, the braves painted their faces with war paint. Cyris had shaved his head, and all the Indians wanted his hair, because it looked like that of the buffalo. He painted his face and scalp red and white and set out with the tribe. They rode and waded through almost knee-high snow all day and half the night.

The Indians planned to launch a surprise attack by catching the soldiers off guard during the middle of the night. They noted that there was a high stockade fence with double gates in its front wall and smaller gates at the rear. Four sentries patrolled the top fenced-in area of the fort with rifles.

Silently, the braves killed the sentries with arrows, while the warriors used ropes to climb over the wall and open the gates. Most of the soldiers were asleep in their quarters. The braves set fire to the men's barracks, killing everyone who rushed out with weapons in hand.

Cyris was in the Indian party out front. He got down on one knee and fired arrows, while the ones behind him used rifles. He fired his bow as fast as he could notch arrows, swiftly bringing down soldiers as they exited the building. When his arrows ran out, he picked up a rifle, looked down the sight, and fired, just as the braves had taught him. They killed everyone except four young women and eight children … including little Christopher. They looted the place, taking all the ammunition and horses.

Cyris found a warm coat, socks, and boots. He saw a gun in its holster and strapped it on. There was a fancy knife in a leather sheath, great for skinning buffaloes, so he grabbed it. He saw a black, wide-brimmed hat on a rack, so he put it on. They ran back to their horses and took off for the village, leaving the blazing fort behind them. They now had more horses than they could ever use.

But Cyris hung back, not wanting to be part of the group that planned to take some of the horses, two of the women, and some of the children to another tribe to trade. He saw the white women huddled together and terrified. It was hard for him to believe they were just wenches and slaves for the Indians, just like black women were for the whites.

***

"Sleeping Buffalo, you don't belong here with these savages," one of the white women said to Cyris while she fetched water from the stream. "We can offer you freedom if you just get us out of here," she begged him.

"See these marks on my back?" he replied. "Indians didn't put them there. I'm free here—not a slave for the white folks." He washed his face in the creek, then said, "Who's calling who a savage anyway?"

"I can set you free," she cried. "Don't you want to be free?"

"Free now, ma'am."

"Find some soldiers and tell them where we are. They'll come for us," she pleaded.

"They'll kill me and everyone in this village," he replied.

"I won't let them hurt you," she promised.

"No," Cyris said. "You call these people savages. White people are the savages. I was here when soldiers from the fort rode in and massacred women and children. White people take land that belongs to the Indians and then kill them because they don't want them around."

"They also attacked and burned people out of their homes, murdered them, and took their scalps," she replied furiously.

"Then don't trespass on their land, ma'am."

She sobbed, "They murdered my husband and took my two children. My daughter is eight, and my son is ten years old."

"I was taken from my mother before I was six. Slaves don't know their parents."

"Where did they take my children?"

"Don't know," Cyris said. He really didn't.

"I'll come to your tipi with you. Be your woman for tonight, if you promise to help me."

Cyris donned his shirt. His voice was wry as he said, "I don't sleep with wenches, ma'am."

"What's your christian name?"

"Sleeping Buffalo," he answered. "That's my name."

"You must have a real name," she said.

"Don't remember," he stated.

Then the woman's face twisted with evil as she hissed at him, "You were with them when they attacked the fort. When the soldiers get here, and they will, I'll make sure you get what you deserve, you black heathen."

"That's exactly what I expected," Cyris said.

He and the Indians were now staunch friends, and no white woman was coming between them with her lies and promises—not if he could help it.

The village waited for soldiers to come, but they never did.

CHAPTER 22

HARD TRAVELS

SPRING HAD FINALLY come. The snow was melting, and flowers would be in bloom soon. It was a bitterly cold morning when Cyris took his sack and all his possessions and rode off on a horse he'd gotten from the fort. He made sure the animal didn't have the Cavalry brand. The Indians didn't want him to leave, but their way of life wasn't for him. And it was just a matter of time before the soldiers came. More than the first group would kill everyone in the village. White folks were like a swarm of locusts that weren't going away.

The last time he saw Christopher, a woman was breastfeeding him.

***

Cyris had a hat, a new coat, a gun, and good directions to Canada. He said thanks and goodbye to everyone and rode off on his own. He placed his bow and arrows in his carrying sack and stuffed his saddlebags with jerky. He buckled his gun belt around his shoulder under his jacket and tucked his knife around his waistband.

None of the folks he met along the way seemed friendly. The first town Cyris rode through, folks stopped and stared at him.

He didn't stop, just kept moving until he found some black folks and asked if he could spend the night. He left his horse tied up outside, ate, and slept in their house. The next morning, his horse was gone. The family said they didn't hear anything during the night, but the only other footprints to where he'd left his horse came from the house. Cyris didn't know it had been a quarter horse until people along the way wanted to purchase it.

It was as Mary said: you can't trust your own folks. Heeding her words, Cyris knew he shouldn't start flashing money around trying to buy another mount, so he left on foot, half-walking, half-running through the woods.

It was a warm day when he stopped at a stream, took a drink, and filled his water pouch. When he stepped back, a moccasin bit him above his ankle inside his leg. Furious, he killed the snake with a stick. In order to save his own life, he used both the white mans' and the Indians' medicines. He sliced an x across the bite and sucked out as much poison possible; then he searched around the forest for the Indian remedy for a snakebite. Quickly, he picked plantain leaves and chewed them into a mash. With trembling hands, he tied the remedy around the bite on his leg with his bandana. He lay on his sleeping rug on the ground and rested, giving the poison time to vent his system. But his leg felt numb, and he became too weak to move. He felt nauseous and had a fever that continued for two days.

Still tired and weary, he took to the main road, seeking help. He met a wagon of four and flagged them down by waving his arms. "Please," he begged. "Can you spare some food?"

"Sure," the woman said. "Betsy, get some beef jerky and this morning's leftover biscuits."

The girl passed the food to Cyris. "This is about all we have."

"Thank you, ma'am. This'll do fine." He didn't have the strength to hunt for a rabbit or catch a fish.

"You need a ride?" the man asked. They were southbound.

"No," Cyris said. He thanked them again and said goodbye.

When the wagon left, he walked back into the forest, gobbled down the food, and fell asleep.

When Cyris woke, it was the middle of the night, and most of his strength had returned. In search of food, he took to the trail again.

At sunup, he met two men on horseback—saddle tramps. He didn't see guns, but they could have been hidden under their jackets.

"Look at what we got here," the tallest one said.

"You a runaway slave, boy?" the other man asked.

Cyris had a bad feeling in the pit of his stomach. "No, suh. I'm on my way to meet my father in the next town."

"What's the name of this town?" the shorter of the two asked.

"Next town, that's all I know."

"What's his name? Your pa?"

Cyris felt his own voice quiver. "Josh."

"No blacks in that town. You're on your way to Canada, ain't you, boy?"

"Where I go ain't none of your mind."

"I think he means it ain't none of our business." The taller one looked at his partner and lowered his head. "Is that what you mean, boy?"

"Wonder how much we can get for him?" the shorter man asked.

"Six, seven hundred dollars. Looks healthy. Good worker."

Knowing there was going to be trouble, Cyris rushed off the trail and into the woods. The men dismounted and followed. A short distance from the trail, Cyris stopped and faced the two men. The shorter man pulled out a knife.

"Hands behind your back, boy," the one holding the knife demanded.

Cyris was eighteen, a man now. The Indians had taught him how to fight with knives, tomahawks, and hand-to-hand combat. If he killed the men, he would be hanged.

When the man came after Cyris with the knife, he pulled a larger knife from the sheath under his jacket. He and the man circled around and around until the man lunged after him. Cyris jumped back.

"Hey. Watch it. We don't want him all cut up," the taller man said.

"Drop that knife, boy," his opponent said.

Cyris gritted his teeth, heart thumping. "You drop yours, or I'm going to carve you up mighty good, mister."

The other man pulled off his jacket, exposing his gun. He wrapped his jacket around his hand and arm and came after Cyris.

Cyris stabbed the man, holding the knife in his neck. Pulling his knife from the man's throat, he threw it, handle first, and it plunged into the other man's chest just as he pulled his gun. The man went limp, the gun fell from his hand, and blood oozed from his mouth.

Cyris removed his knife from the man's chest, wiped it on the dead man's jacket, and placed it back into its sheath. Retrieving his hat, he walked back into the trail without firing a shot.

***

It took him the rest of the summer to reach about halfway across Michigan. Unlike New Orleans, it was starting to get cold very early.

A white man driving a loaded wagon with a team of four horses offered Cyris a ride. He was going about twelve miles to make a delivery.

Cyris hopped on the front seat. "Thank you, suh. Somebody stole my horse a way's back."

"You're headed to Canada, ain't you, son?"

"Just traveling," Cyris said.

"Why don't you buy another horse?"

"Can't afford a horse," Cyris said. "Unless I steal one, and that's a hanging offense."

When the man reached his final destination, he summoned the sheriff, who was standing in the street, talking with a woman.

"Sheriff," the man called. "I picked this boy up on the trail. I think he's a runaway from the South."

"Get down off that wagon," the sheriff demanded.

Cyris stepped down with his sack in hand.

"What you got in that sack?" the sheriff asked.

"Just personal things," Cyris said, realizing that his freedom, and possibly his life, as he'd planned it were coming to a bad end. How could he explain the money, the bow and arrows hidden in his sack, or the gun belt under his jacket?

"Dump everything on the ground," the sheriff ordered.

Cyris could already feel the rope around his neck. How could he explain carrying more money than these folks would ever see in their entire lives? If he pulled out his pistol and started shooting, the entire state of Michigan would be after him. With him being black and easy to spot, they were bound to catch him.

People had now started to gather. One man rode up on his horse and curiously slid off the animal.

Grabbing his bag, Cyris swiftly jumped on the horse and galloped north.

"Stop," the sheriff yelled, "or I'll shoot."

Cyris heard a shot fired into the air, but he continued out of town on a slow horse. Riding hard, he looked back and saw four men gaining fast behind him. When he entered a bend in the road, he abruptly stopped the horse, jumped off, slapped it on its rear, and the horse continued to gallop away. Using an old Indian trick, Cyris wiped his footprints off the trail with a branch and ran into the woods. He continued north but stayed clear of roads and trails. He spent three nights in the freezing weather without a fire. On the fourth day, he killed a rabbit with his bow and arrow and cooked it over an open fire. The sheriff wouldn't spend much time seeking a runaway slave. He'd probably given up and was already back home, sitting in front of a warm fire.

***

Each night seemed colder than the one before. One night while trekking through light snow, Cyris saw a glow in the dark and headed toward it.

Three men were lying on their upside-down saddles around a fire.

Cyris cautiously moved in. "Hello, men. Can you spare some food and your fire?" he asked in the most sympathetic voice he could muster.

All three men sat up.

"We have company," the bearded man said. He wasn't the largest, but he was the tallest of the three.

A young man about Cyris's age stood and threw two sticks of wood on the fire. "You lost?"

Cyris knew he had made a mistake. He lowered his head and started walking away. "I'll move along."

"You got any money?" the kid asked.

"No, suh."

"You're from the South," the bearded man said, standing. "What are you doing so far from home? Ran away, did you?"

"No, suh. I'm a free man."

"Why are you wearing buckskins?" the largest man asked.

"I lived with the Indians for a spell."

"You help them redskins kill white folks, boy?" the big man asked.

"No, suh. Never went on no raiding party. Just stayed in the village. They shared their food with me."

"Is that what you're expecting us to do? Share our food?" The bearded man stepped forward.

"Yes, suh. Had nothing to eat for days."

"Thought about looking for a job?" the kid asked.

"I've worked for food, here and there."

"Well, you better find yourself another one of them jobs, because we ain't sharing nothing with you, even our fire. Now git," the kid said.

"Hold it. Hold it," the largest man said. "Let's see what he's carrying in that sack. Looks a little bulky just for clothes."

Cyris pulled out his bow and arrow. "It's just for hunting rabbits."

"What happened? Couldn't find a rabbit?" the man with the beard asked.

"If I find a rabbit, can I sleep here tonight?"

"We've had dinner." The younger man jumped toward Cyris, grabbed his sack, and dumped out its contents.

With awe in his voice, he said, "Look at all this cash." He picked up one stack, tore one of the strings off, and thumbed through the bills.

The other two closed in, eyes bulging. "And there's more."

"Where did you get all this money from, boy?"

Cyris struggled to reply. "I—"

"Don't matter where he got it from. It's ours now," the largest man said.

"Put that back," Cyris warned.

"You talking to us, boy?" the youngest man asked.

The kid punched Cyris in the face, and he lurched back from the impact. The next punch got Cyris in his stomach.

"He has something under his jacket," the kid said, shaking his fist.

The two older men held Cyris's arms while the youngest one pounded him in his face.

Then they shoved him to the ground. "Stand up and take off that jacket."

Cyris leaped up and landed a fist into the jaw of the bearded man, who reeled and fell backward. The largest man pulled out his pistol from under his jacket, but Cyris kicked it from his hand, then punched him in the face as well.

The youngest man came up behind Cyris and jumped on his back. The bearded man recovered and came after Cyris again, but Cyris ducked, and the man's huge fist landed on his younger partner's face.

The tallest man pulled a pistol from beneath his jacket. A loud bang roared throughout the night, and Cyris felt a burning pain in his arm. Diving for the pistol lying a few feet away, Cyris grabbed it, rolled over, and fired several shots in rapid succession, killing all three men within seconds.

Cyris checked his wounded arm. The bullet had passed through the muscle. He removed his jacket and buckskin shirt, patched up his wound with a bandana, and used his mouth and free hand to tie it tight to mitigate the bleeding. Quickly, he stuffed his things back into his sack, mounted one of the horses, and galloped north. He rode for the remainder of the night. Stopping at the edge of a small town in the dark, he dismounted and walked right through as fast as he could.

CHAPTER 23

THE UNDERGROUND RAILROAD

"STRAIGHT NORTH. FOLLOW the North Star."

That's what Mary had told him.

He traveled mostly at night, passing through towns as quickly as possible. Trouble could be lurking anywhere. People shared their food here and there, but caution caused him to go hungry most of the time. He didn't have many small bills, and he wanted to keep them. He stopped at a small-town mercantile and bought a pair of pants to wear over his buckskin trousers and a pair of gloves. The woman stared at him all the while she made change. Why, he didn't even know if the amount of change she gave him was correct. He could count, but he was so nervous, he didn't bother. He made it to the next town about nightfall, stopped an old black man on the street, and asked where he could spend the night.

"You need to find a family. No hotel will rent you a

room. Miss Emily has a house all to herself. You probably can spend the night there, if'n you can pay. I'll take you there. It's too cold to sleep outside tonight, son. Watch where you go here. There are white men who'll take you down South and sell you, even if'n you free."

The old man walked him a short distance to a run-down house and knocked on the door.

"Who's there?" a woman called out.

"It's me, Miss Emily. I have a house guest for you."

When the door opened, Cyris saw the faint light from a lamp in the background. Other than that, the place was dark. He could barely make out the woman's face, but he saw she was black, although her voice sounded white to him.

A wood heater was burning in the center of the room. Blankets and quilts covered the divan, as if the woman slept there to keep warm during the night. She wore a thick robe over her clothes.

"Who're you? Come in, so I can get a look at you." She opened the door wider. The woman looked about fifty. Like the old man, she hadn't been worth taking down to the South to sell.

The old man remained outside as Cyris stepped inside. The room was warm and cozy, and he didn't want to leave it.

"Hello, Miss Emily. My name's Cyris. I really need a place to stay tonight, and I'm freezing cold."

"I'll let you two get acquainted," the old man said. "Goodnight, folks."

Miss Emily closed the door and led Cyris to the heater, where he removed his gloves. He dropped his sack on the floor and removed his jacket.

The woman gasped, "You have a gun and a knife? Black folks can't have those things."

"I've been traveling for miles with my weapons. They're no trouble, which is why I hide them under my jacket."

"You need to get rid of them. Do you know what white folks will do to you if they catch you with weapons? Call you a murderer and a thief and probably hang you. You'll be charged for any murder or robbery within a hundred miles of here."

"What do you suggest I do with them, leave them outside the door? If you're turning me out, you have the right, but my weapons go with me," Cyris said. He donned his jacket and picked up his sack. "I'll just have to survive in the cold for another night."

"Have you killed anyone?" she asked.

"No, and I don't care to discuss where I got these. Nothing illegal," he assured her, walking toward the door.

"Why, you're just a boy. You hungry, young man?"

Cyris grinned, relaxing a little. "Yes, ma'am. I could eat a horse about now."

He got a better look at the room. It reminded him of his old slave quarters, except the floor was pinewood rather than dirt. The place had windows and furniture. The room smelled nice, and it was clean.

"All right, you can spend the night here. But I want you gone in the morning."

"Yes, ma'am."

"Put that gun in your bag."

When Cyris pulled out his bow to make room for the gun, the woman gasped again. "Where did you get that?"

"From the Indians. I use it to kill rabbits."

She shook her head. "My, my ..."

"If you don't trust me, you can keep them."

"I will not," she said. "How old are you?"

"Eighteen."

"How long you been traveling?"

"Almost a year."

"You got family?" Miss Emily asked.

"Don't know where they are. I was born a slave."

"You're a mighty brave boy. Determined."

The woman dumped some flour into a bowl and sat a pan of sliced pork belly on the heater.

"Were you ever a slave, Miss Emily?"

"When I was eleven, my mother ran off with me, and this is as far as we got. You see, my mother got sick and couldn't make the rest of the trip. I worked as a maid to keep us in food. One of the ladies I worked for let us live here for free, since we didn't have a roof over our heads. When the woman died, she left us this house in her will. Her children didn't like the idea, but they didn't bother us. They let us be."

"Any brothers and sisters?"

"They were a lot older than me, and they were sold off at about ten or eleven years old. That's why my mother headed to Canada."

The woman fried up pork belly in one skillet and a hoecake in another. Just the smell made Cyris want to beg for food. He poured syrup on the bread and greedily gulped it down while she brought him a cup of hot tea. "Sure is good, ma'am."

She stared at him as he ate. "You need to learn how to use utensils rather than eating with your hands. You're from the South; people can tell, you know. Keep your mouth closed when you chew, so you don't smack your lips. Headed to Canada?"

He didn't want to admit it, but he had to trust someone. He licked his fingers. "Yes, ma'am."

"I'm not asking exactly where you're from, because it's none of my business. I can get you to Canada safely. You're almost there. Lucky you made it this far without being caught."

"I've had my problems along the way."

"Stay here for another day. I'll see what I can do about getting you to your destination."

"How can you do that?"

"Ever heard of the Underground Railroad?" she asked.

"No, ma'am, but I've heard there are people who will help folks like me escape to freedom."

"We help black people like you travel east or north to

Canada. You can live here, but white folks might kidnap you and sell you back to the South."

"How did you manage to stay here so long?"

"When we first moved here, we were live-in maids in a large house for about ten years. We never left the house unless we were with one of the occupants or in a crowded place. Even now, I don't like going out at night."

"Why didn't you move on to Canada?"

"After my mother died, I thought about it. A man came through on his way. We got married, and he got a job. A week later, he disappeared."

"He was sold back to the South?"

"I guess. I've been lucky living here. I wasn't worth as much as a male. And white folks looked after me because I've worked for most of them at some time or another. I'm honest and trustworthy. Never stole anything."

***

Cyris spent two days at Miss Emily's house catching up on needed sleep. He hadn't realized how exhausted he was.

He paid the woman a dollar a day for room and board.

Without warning, she said, "We leave tonight. If you can give some money for our cause, please do. We use it to buy food and clothes for those who can't afford it. If you don't have any money, that's all right too. We'll still get you to Canada. We leave about midnight. You ready to travel, son?"

"Ain't I free here?" he asked. "I can live careful like you do."

"Canada is safer if you can stand the cold winters."

"It's colder than here?"

"Depends on where you end up. Just across the border, the weather is about the same as here. At least, that's what I hear. When you move to Canada, travel a distance from the border. You'll be safer there. Once you become a Canadian citizen, it's illegal—and harder—to transport you back here."

Cyris was afraid. He knew he couldn't trust anyone. Maybe she and her friends planned to rob him blind or sell him back to the South. "Why so late?"

"Most people are in bed by then, and it's hard to tell what color folks are at night. We have to walk to the next town. I'll turn you over to someone else there, and they will take you a distance. Tell no one. Not even in a letter. You know how to read and write?"

"A few words. I can read and write my name real good," he said proudly.

"When you reach your final destination, learn how to read and write. Don't mention the name Canada again, even to me. It's your final destination. Got it, son?"

"Yes, ma'am."

During his stay with Miss Emily, Cyris made a pouch and stuffed most of his money around his waist, keeping the small bills in his pocket. When midnight came, he felt anxious and afraid. Even if he made it to his final destination, what would he do there? He'd never thought about that before.

Cyris and Miss Emily walked through the woods all night without a lantern, arriving at another house in the country. The rundown barn was in the same condition as Miss Emily's house. They didn't go into the nicer house but took shelter in the barn and slept under warm quilts in the hayloft. Cyris had just fallen asleep when the barn door squeaked open. "Anybody up there?" a voice demanded.

"It's me. I brought you a guest. A young man," Miss Emily said.

"Come on down. He can help me hook up the team," the man said.

When Cyris climbed down the ladder behind Miss Emily, he saw a black man dressed like a cowboy: hat, boots—the whole works. He looked about forty. Walking toward Cyris, he extended his hand and tightly squeezed Cyris's.

"Hey, they call me Western on account of the way I dress." He flashed white teeth in a wide grin. "You're going to help me with a shipment. I drive a wagon to a town about a hundred miles north of here. I'll enjoy your company on the road. We have to camp out, but don't worry. We'll have plenty of blankets and quilts to keep us warm."

"I'm Cyris," he said, then pressed a twenty-dollar gold piece into Miss Emily's palm. It was his only coin. "Thanks, lady. I appreciate your kindness."

She didn't look at the coin, just stuffed it into her pocket. "Have a safe trip."

Miss Emily climbed back into the hayloft while Cyris helped hook up a team of four horses.

"A train don't go this route, so I haul freight up there. We do about twenty-five miles a day. We make better time if we have a light load. Plus, I get fresh horses at the relay stations."

"You haul stuff back as well?"

"Sure, son. An empty wagon don't pay nothing."

"What do you haul?"

"Whatever people want. Sometimes it's lumber, dry goods, even food." He chuckled. "Once, I hauled a whole load of ladies' hats, dropping off orders here and there."

Western drove the team to a mill where two black men loaded up his wagon with windows.

Western introduced him. "This is Cyris. He's the son of a friend."

After the wagon was loaded, Cyris hopped into the seat with Western. "You taking this load all the way?" he asked.

"Yep. Can't pick up nothing else along the way, unless they're ladies' hats," the man chuckled.

Western was the most talkative companion he'd traveled with so far.

"Are you free?" Cyris asked.

"Yes. Carry my papers everywhere I go. Bought a wallet just for that purpose. Just fold it over once and slip it inside. I would buy my kinfolk and bring them up here, but I don't know who or where they are. Gets kind of lonesome sometimes."

"Where and when were you ever a slave?"

Western grinned. "Georgia, for the first twenty-six years of my life."

"How did you get your freedom?"

"My master's gardener accidentally got himself killed when a tree fell on him. There was this huge tree at the mansion, and the master wanted it cut down. The gardener didn't see the tree fall until it was too late. It didn't go in the direction he'd planned. I was temporarily gardener until they could hire someone else. They had a summer house on the lake, not too far from the plantation. The master was trying to teach his twelve-year-old son responsibilities. The kid stuffed the fireplace with wood, so he wouldn't have to get up in the middle of the night. A spark from the fireplace set the house ablaze. Everyone was asleep. It was in the middle of the night when I woke up and saw the house engulfed in flames. I ran over, opened the front door, and yelled, 'Fire.' By that time, the fire had just about consumed the entire house. My master and his wife were asleep in the front room. It was easier for them to escape, but their son and six-year-old daughter were in the back bedrooms. I risked my life. Got burned pretty badly, too, but I managed to get the kids out of there with only minor burns."

"I don't see any burns on you."

"My scalp, back, and arms. That's why I wear a hat all the time."

"And he set you free?"

"Yep. I headed North. Came here with two hundred dollars in my pocket that the master gave me. I worked for a while, saved my money, and started my own business. You can do the same thing, no matter where you end up. Be respectable, let people get to know that you're kind and honest."

"I don't know how to do anything," Cyris said.

"I didn't either until I started working for a freight company, hauling things. Then I got to thinking. Why don't I go into business for myself? Now I'm my old boss's main competitor."

"So, I need to learn a trade?"

"You got it, young man."

"How did you know to move North?"

"Word gets around on a plantation if you keep your ear to the wall. Actually, I had planned to run away."

"Slaves on plantations usually don't know what's going on outside," Cyris said. "I didn't until I made friends with someone who did."

"Most don't—don't know because they don't want to know. They've had someone else tell them when to get up in the mornings, what to do, and when to go to bed all their lives. They don't have to worry about where their next meal is coming from. It's provided."

"I didn't know either until my friend informed me."

"Where is he?"

"She's dead. Her name was Mary."

"Sorry to hear that, son. She must have been special."

"She was," Cyris said. "Once I'm free, I'm going to buy her little sister."

"There was this girl who was teaching us kids how to read and write," Western said. "One of the master's children taught her."

"She taught you how to read?"

"It was a start. The kids didn't tell, but the grown-ups did. They ratted her out."

"What did they do to her?"

"They hanged her," Western said. "Fifteen years old, and they hanged her as an example. That's how slave owners control us, through ignorance and fear—ignorance because they don't want us to know how to read or what's going on in the world about freedom outside the plantation. Using fear by making an example of people who try to do better by whipping, torturing, or hanging. Learn, Cyris. Read and learn everything you can. Only ignorance can keep you down. I have books at my place that I've read ten times or more."

"I will," Cyris said. "You ever thought about getting married?"

"Ain't no black women around here my age. I've met a few good-looking ones passing through. None wanted to stay."

Cyris knew what he meant. The women were on their way to Canada.

"After I settled down here and got to know folks, they stopped bothering me. They mind their business, and I mind mine."

He walked the horses until sundown, then let them graze in a nearby meadow near a stream and fed each of them a bucket of oats. They set up camp there, sleeping on the ground.

The next morning, they had pig belly with biscuits and syrup. Cyris helped hitch the team, and they lit out at dawn.

"At least there's still grass so the horses can graze," Western said. "During the snowy months, it's hard to make this trip. I can always buy hay from a relay station, but the horses can't pull the wagon through deep snow. I got snowed in one year."

"What did you do then?" Cyris asked.

Western chuckled. "If I had enough sense, I wouldn't try to make deliveries in bad weather, but much of my business is during the winter months. Some freight companies don't deliver, due to the snow."

"Why do you do it?"

"As I mentioned earlier, I'm the only black freight operator in these parts. I had to build up people's trust and confidence in me. I'll make the trip when others won't. It gets me more business."

"What do you do when the snow gets too deep to travel?"

"I try to make it to a relay station for feed and shelter

for the horses. I sleep in the barn. Not allowed to sleep inside with white folks, you know. I've met a few black folks who'll put me up too. When the snow starts to melt, I move on."

"What if you can't make it to a relay station?"

"I carry a shovel with me. I dig out a place off the road, unhitch the team, and wait it out."

"What about food for the horses?"

"During the winter, I always carry two extra sacks of oats. The horses don't starve; I do."

At the end of the journey, Cyris helped Western unload the windows at a place called Brady Lumber and Furniture. Western took him to another place where he traded the horses for a fresh team. While there, he introduced Cyris to a black man named Claudius. The man didn't seem as friendly or trustworthy, but Cyris had no choice in the matter. He helped Claudius at the relay station for the rest of the day and followed him home. He had a wife and five children who lived not far from his place of employment. The man seemed sad or disappointed with his life. He rarely talked, even with his own family.

"Can you pay for your room and board?" Claudius asked once they made it to his place.

"How much you asking?" Cyris asked.

"A dollar a night, plus anything you can give for the cause," he said.

"How long will I remain here?" Cyris asked.

"Just tonight," Claudius answered.

Cyris gave him a five-dollar bill, the smallest thing he had. He didn't give more, because he didn't want anyone to think he had money. "I don't have much left. Just hope I can find a job at my final destination."

"I can only promise you two things—you won't starve or be a slave there."

Cyris slept on a mattress on the floor with a nine-month-old baby who kicked his feet, squealed, and made goo-goo-gaa-gaa noises most of the night. Cyris didn't mind his young bed companion.

The next morning, he stood about a mile from the re-lay station, where he waited for his next ride.

A young white man pulled his wagon to a halt and asked, "You Cyris? I'm David."

Claudius had told him the man's name but never said he was white. Cyris was sure his journey to freedom was over. He stood in his tracks, scared out of his wits. He wanted to run but didn't know where to go. He shud-dered. "I can find my own way. Thank you."

"I don't blame you for being cautious," David said. "But I've helped slaves in the past escape to Canada."

"Why would you help me?" Cyris asked.

"Not all white people believe in slavery. I don't. Many of the people who support the Underground Railroad are white like me."

Cyris was still skeptical but climbed aboard. "How far are you going?"

"About sixty miles," David said. "I travel the distance once a month to see my parents and sister."

"I was told that some people take black men back down to the South and sell them. You're not afraid of driving with me?" Cyris asked.

"I carry a shotgun on the floorboard. Travel only during the day and stay over with another family during the trip. I see nobody's kidnapped you yet," David said.

"I've had a few close calls."

"How did you get away?" David asked.

"I used my fists. The Indians taught me how to fight real dirty."

David laughed. "You lived with the Indians?"

"All last winter. They taught me how to hunt and live off the land."

"I've heard that they scalp and torture people."

"Only white people," Cyris said. "They were real nice to me. The only time they took my hair was when I shaved my head."

"Other than visiting my folks, I never go far from my house with company."

"You married?" Cyris asked.

"Got a wife and two sons. One is six months old; the other is two."

"What do you do here?" Cyris asked.

"Blacksmith. I'm supposed to be partners with this man, but he takes most of the money. I learned the trade and became a better blacksmith than him."

"Why don't you start your own business?"

"I am. In the town where my parents live. There's one there, but he's unreliable. Drinks a lot."

"When are you moving?"

"Next summer, when my kids can travel. I've found a building, and I'm buying it. The bank even gave me a loan. I'm trying to pay it back as fast as I can."

"You make lots of money?"

"Sometimes when customers come into the shop, I pocket the money. It's mine anyway."

"You put money into this man's shop?"

"Every penny I owned. Didn't get it legal, on paper. Never trust people, Cyris."

***

About sundown, David knocked on the door of a fancy house, and a white man answered.

"Hello, David. Who's your friend?"

"Jake, this is Cyris. We need to spend the night here, if it's all right with you."

"Come on in." Jake lowered his voice. "Nice to meet you, Cyris. My folks are up there in age. They go to bed very early. I live here and take care of them."

David said, "We haven't had anything to eat all day, Jake."

"Come on in the kitchen. I'll make you some sandwiches. You all have to vacate the premises before my parents wake up in the morning. They don't believe in our cause, being from the South."

That was the first time Cyris had eaten at a table with white men. He got another good night's sleep and didn't want to get out of his soft bed that next morning, but he had no choice.

Shortly after dawn, Cyris and David hit the road again, arriving at David's parent's house about sundown. They stopped at a placed on the outskirts of town and unhitched the team in a small barn.

David knocked on the door. "Mom, it's me."

A woman about mid-fifties opened the door and hugged David. "Hello, son. Who's this?"

The smell of food made Cyris hungry. "My name is Cyris, ma'am."

"Come on in. Will you be spending the night, Cyris?"

"Yes, he will, Mom. Where's Dad?"

"Working late. Expecting him home any minute now."

A girl walked into the living room. She seemed slow and a bit awkward. "David." She gave her brother a tight hug. "Can't wait until you move back here. I want to play with the kids."

"Cyris, this is my sister, Ann."

"Hello, Ann. Nice to meet you."

"You David's friend?" Ann asked.

"Sort of."

The door opened, and a man walked in. "I told you to

keep this door locked, honey. David, we weren't expecting you to bring a friend."

"This is Cyris, Dad. He'll be spending the night."

"Dinner is about ready. Let's go into the kitchen," David's mother said.

"Smells good, ma'am," Cyris said.

"My mom is the best cook in this town. She used to cook at the restaurant."

"Okay, you men. Get washed up before dinner," David's mother said.

They sat down to a meal of pot roast, mashed potatoes, carrots, and dinner rolls.

Cyris didn't want to eat like a pig, but he couldn't help himself. "This is mighty good grub, ma'am."

"Want some more?" she asked.

"Couldn't eat another bite," Cyris replied. He even offered to wash the dishes out of sheer gratitude for his full belly.

"That's woman's work. Ann and I will take care of the kitchen. You men go into the living room and get acquainted."

Cyris enjoyed David's family. He knew he'd really missed out on knowing his own folks, his own kin. They gave him a warm, loving feeling and a sense of belonging.

They just didn't know how lucky they were.

The next day, David drove Cyris to another town and introduced him to a black family: Ida, Willis, and their two children. It had started to snow, and Cyris hoped

David would make it back home before nightfall. David didn't ask for money, just wished him good luck.

At least a foot of snow had accumulated during the night, and it was still coming down hard. Cyris spent a week with the family of four until he could travel. He shoveled snow from the front of stores and businesses and sometimes worked overtime to avoid the fighting at home.

Ida was a nag, and Willis had a woman on the side, according to his wife. Cyris didn't like living there because the couple fought all the time—not just verbally but with hand-to-hand combat. The young kids were afraid and cried all the time. Cyris did all he could to avoid getting into their disagreements.

When Cyris arrived home about eight o'clock that night, something crashed against the opposite wall. A lamp fell from the table, broke into pieces, and the spilled oil started a fire. Rather than control the situation, the couple continued fighting with the fire blazing in the background.

"Ouch," Willis yelled. "You just bit me."

"That's for slapping my face, you pig."

Cyris put out the fire with a bucket of water and threw a blanket over it.

The six-year-old girl stood in the doorway of her bedroom. "Is our house going to burn down?"

"No, honey. I just put out the fire."

"Our neighbor's house burned down, and they lost everything," she cried.

"See what you did," Willis yelled. "Started a fire and almost put us on the street."

Willis slapped Ida's face again. She fell backward, smashed into the wall, and slid to the floor.

She immediately bounced to her feet and went after him, digging her fingernails into his face and neck. Willis then punched her. Her head snapped back, but she took the blow like a man. She pounced on him again, this time hitting him with her fists, busting his lip.

"Stop it," Cyris finally yelled. "You're supposed to help people like me reach freedom. Your kids are afraid and crying. You almost just burned down your own house. I can't stay here anymore."

They both stopped fighting and stared at Cyris as if he were insane.

Cyris walked into the boy's room, collected his sack, and walked out the front door, never looking back. One of the buildings he'd shoveled that day had an overhang with a slight shelter from the wind. He huddled underneath it with his sleeping robe wrapped around himself, trying to keep warm. He had never been so cold in his life, and he understood Canada was colder than this. Maybe he should head for New York City instead. He saw a lantern moving toward him.

"Who's there?" a man called out.

"I'm waiting for the morning stage," Cyris said.

"There's a boarding house down the street." The man moved closer and got a better look at Cyris. "It's too cold to spend the night out here. I'm the sheriff. Come down to the jail. I have empty bunks in there where you can sleep."

The last place Cyris wanted to go was a jail. "I'll wait here, if you don't mind. I don't want to be a bother."

"Nonsense, get your bag and come along."

Cyris trembled due to the cold weather and fear, but he did as the sheriff said. He picked up his sack, clutched his sleeping rug in his arm, and followed the sheriff into a nearby, dimly-lit jail. It wasn't that warm, but it was out of the wind.

The sheriff lit another lamp and led him into the back. "Pick a bunk, doesn't matter which one."

Sheer terror rippled through Cyris's body, and his eyes grew wide. "You're going to lock me up?"

"No," the man said. "The doors are open."

Cyris never removed his jacket, just lay down and didn't wake up until the next morning when the sheriff banged a tin coffee cup on the bars. "Time to get up," he said. "Stage leaves here in thirty minutes. Got some eggs and bacon cooking. Eat before you leave."

"Thanks for letting me sleep here, suh. I was mighty tired."

Cyris gobbled down his food and drank his coffee. "Want me to wash the dishes?" he offered.

"No. Have a safe trip, son," the man said.

He purchased a ticket and rode on top of the coach with the driver.

Wearing his buckskins under his jacket, he wrapped his sleeping robe around himself to help protect against the pre-dawn chill. His body felt as if it were an icicle. He was happy to see the stars fading from sight and morning nearing. It took them five days to reach Detroit.

Not knowing where to go, he followed the other passengers inside the stage depot. He didn't see a line for black people, so he stood behind an elderly white couple.

When he took his turn at the counter, he said to the man dressed in black. "I'd like to buy a ticket to Canada."

"Where in Canada are you going?" the man asked.

"What's the next town?" Cyris asked nervously.

"You can walk there. Won't cost you a thing."

Cyris stuttered, "How far will ten dollars take me?"

"You want to go to a city or a small town?"

"Small town. Countryside," he said.

"All right. How about Raven?"

"That's fine," Cyris said.

This time he rode inside with two other passengers. He knew Canada was nearby, but he didn't realize how close until he looked up and saw a sign that read: "Welcome to Canada."

Made in the USA
Columbia, SC
29 June 2020